SPECTRAL CROSSINGS

MICHAEL McBRIDE

snowbooks

Proudly Published by Snowbooks in 2009

Snowbooks Ltd.
120 Pentonville Road
London
N1 9JN
Tel: 0207 837 6482
Fax: 0207 837 6348
email: info@snowbooks.com
www.snowbooks.com

British Library Cataloguing in Publication Data
A catalogue record for this book is available from the British
Library.

Printed by J. H. Haynes & Co. Ltd., Sparkford

ISBN 13 978-1-905005-91-8

To Anna, Em, and Rob

SPECTRAL CROSSINGS

Dark for fear of failure
An inner gloom as wide as an eye and
fermenting
Roiling hate
Death grip in my veins
Unveiling rancid petals
Flowering forth foul nectar
The space between a blink and a tear
... Death Blooms

— Mudvayne
"Death Blooms"

CHAPTER 1

RAIN OF BLOOD

I

"Don't make a sound, or it'll hear you," Brian whispered. "Not a sound."

He seized his younger brother by the shoulders and drove him to his knees in the flowing water.

"What about you?" Steve screamed up from the mire, rainwater dragging his bangs down his forehead.

"Don't worry about me," he said, shoving Steve backwards into the drainage pipe that cut through the mounded earth beneath the dirt road. "I'll go find help. You hide in this pipe, hear me? No matter what you see, don't come out. Understand? Don't come out!"

Steve caught a transient reflection from the water that covered his brother's features, limning his face like the shimmering silver of a trout's scales.

Brian's hand shot from his side and landed squarely in the middle of Steve's face, fingers fanned around his wide, startled eyes. With one final push, Brian forced his brother back into the darkness of the tunnel, then whirled and splashed back into the marsh.

Thunder grumbled across the sky like a truck grinding over a gravel road.

Steve cringed and nipped a strap of soft flesh from the inside of his lower lip.

"Brian," Steve whimpered, but he couldn't even hear his own voice over the patter of rain on the stream.

He ducked back into the tube and scooted farther and farther backwards, until he could barely make out the circular opening, let alone what lie in wait without.

"Please, Brian," he cried, his shoulders shaking uncontrollably. "I don't want to die…"

II

"I bet he killed her," Brian had said, tossing his dirt bike aside into the bushes. "Probably stabbed her, like, thirty times and weighted her down with some big rocks."

Steve hadn't wanted to come in the first place. Not after what had happened here.

They hadn't even found her body.

"You know Dad's going to kill us when he finds out that we came down here," Steve said. He almost wished their father's old, rust-eaten Suburban would come bounding down the washboard road, with an angry fist of dust rising from beneath its mud-crusted flaps. They may have been in serious trouble, but at least their old man would have dragged them home. Away from here, anyway.

"How's he going to find out?" Brian slung his creel from around his back to hang beside his hip, like a purse that reeked of sun-warmed fish guts. The Indian arrowhead he wore around his neck on a length of stretched leather flopped out from beneath his shirt. The polished surface reflected the sunlight from the chiseled serrations toward the tip. "We're not going to tell him, right?"

Steve hesitated.

"Oh, you'd better not!" Brian snapped. His fist struck like a rattler, tagging Steve soundly in the shoulder with a solid thump.

"Ow!" Steve grabbed his throbbing shoulder and massaged the pain from the knuckle dents that were already beginning to turn a sickly manila. He wanted nothing more than to scream into his brother's face and throw him to the ground and see how much *he* liked being beaten, but in the end—as was always the case—crocodile tears swelled over his lashes.

"For God's sake," Brian huffed, rolling his eyes.

"Just leave me alone."

"I'm sorry," Brian sighed, biting his lower lip. Steve's cooperation was the only way he was going to be able to pull this thing off. Had he left his younger brother at home alone, his parents would have tanned his hide. *How dare you leave Steven all alone!* he could hear them saying. *He's only eleven! You're fourteen! You're supposed to be the responsible one!*

Steve looked up at his older brother through shimmering eyes.

Brian forged a smile, but filled it with too many teeth. His jaw muscles pulsed.

"Why do you always have to be such a jerk?" Steve whined.

"Someone's gotta toughen you up," Brian said, clapping his brother on the shoulder.

III

They left their bikes beneath a stand of cottonwoods just off the road, in a weather-beaten patch of mud, thick with the ridges left by all of the cars that had been parked there over the course of the last week. There wasn't a single vehicle there now, but there were a handful of crumpled Styrofoam cups in the underbrush and cigarette butts stamped into the turf. There were even spots where the yellow police tape hung from the trunks of trees, thin tendrils of yellow wriggling against the bark in the breeze.

Clusters of willows crowded around the far larger cottonwoods, filling the space beneath the lower canopy of the spade-leafed behemoths. Parting the wall of leaves and branches, Brian shoved through along the path, watching his toes so they didn't snag under any of the aggressive roots that rose from the mud. One hand shielded his eyes from the branches that clawed at his face; the other clutched the creel to keep it from being snared.

Steve followed, staying right on his brother's heels to keep from getting swatted with the branches when they whipped suddenly back into place.

As recently as the day before, the entire lake had been overrun by cops in yellow slickers and hoods. The majority had tramped through the underbrush, while scuba divers plunged into the middle of the lake from a large gray inflatable raft. No one had been allowed to get close, least of all the handful of residents that surrounded the lake in their modest-sized ranch homes. All they really knew at first was that there had been about a dozen cop cars packed in that small lot and a pair of officers stationed in the middle of the road in orange vests, waving road flares. News vans had been parked haphazardly on the slanted shoulder, the satellite dishes on their roofs fully extended. Camera crews worked at the side of the road, trying to get a clear shot of the lake, though the night had been bereft of anything but the faintest starlight, muted by the trailing edge of the storm.

Their father had driven them down there that first night, or at least as close as they could get, and they had just sat there in the car, watching the huge halide spotlights sweeping across the deep, black water. Only the divers' heads would surface, shaking in frustration, before diving back down into the depths. Invisible hounds barked from the underbrush as they led harried officers through the dense reeds.

By morning, word had spread that Melinda Wright hadn't come home the night before. Worse, Kyle Weatherly, her boyfriend since their junior year of high school, had slipped into his house in the middle of the night without waking his parents and gone straight out to the garage. Sometime between eleven thirty and midnight, Kyle had pressed his forehead to the barrel of his father's twelve-gauge, his thumb on the trigger, and blasted brain-coated steel pellets right through the ceiling, into his parents' bedroom above.

IV

The water had yet to recede from that ferocious storm. The thin paths through the groves of willows and cottonwoods were flooded like troughs, and the fields of cattails that encompassed every last remaining inch of space stood in the runoff. Splashing through the muddy water, they followed the path as best they could, occasionally catching glimpses of the sunlight reflecting from the distant lake, through reeds that were even taller than they were. A solitary mallard quacked a monotonous, droning call from somewhere beside them. Starlings flapped from one tree to the next, mirroring their progress as though stalking them from the enclaves of leaves.

They had to marvel at just how thick and lush the marshland was all around them. They could have walked right beside a body and never have known.

At long last the cattails peeled back to either side, making way for the sloppy bank and pristine lake that stretched off toward the horizon.

Kettner Lake certainly wasn't the world's largest. With a heavy lure, Brian could cast a third of the way across it. On a late August afternoon following a heavy rain, the bass would be willing to strike at just about anything they threw out there.

"You think she's under there?" Brian asked, surveying the blessedly tranquil surface, reflecting the pale blue sky above. Wisps of white cottony clouds swirled in the middle, growing grayer and more ominous toward the opposite shore. "You know…maybe she just sank down into the mud on the bottom."

Steve didn't share his brother's morbid obsession, but it hadn't been a moment prior that he had chased that exact same thought from the back of his mind.

"They didn't find her," Brian stated plainly. "Dan Martin said his dad told him they dredged the bottom every day. They even had those bloodhounds out here sniffing through the swamp for her. And still nothing."

Steve assembled his rod from the carrying case and tried not to pat attention to what Brian was saying.

"It was raining really hard that night. You know how those flash floods just come crashing down from the foothills, dragging all sorts of mud and branches.

Could have buried her way down there in a hurry."

Kicking off his sneakers, Steve padded barefoot across the muddy bank, careful to avoid the black and white piles of duck and goose feces.

"One day," Brian said, softer, as if merely thinking aloud. "One day…maybe not this year or the next… someone's going to cast out there into the water and hook themselves a shred of her clothing. Or the water level will drop, and bones will start washing up on shore."

Steve waded out through the sapling cottonwoods with their red-stemmed, sunburst leaves, careful not to create too much of a stir as he slurped his feet out of the soggy muck. The tip of his raised rod arched back, and then snapped forward. A lone splash marred the otherwise virgin surface of the lake.

"You know what happened to her," Brian whispered to the ripples that rolled gently toward the bank. "You're just not telling."

V

Time lost all meaning there in the shallows as they hauled in fish hand over fist. The small-mouths were tagging the minnow lures like they hadn't eaten in weeks. Probably hadn't, with all of the ruckus around the lake recently. But every time they reeled in a fish, they were forced to pry the hook from deep within its jaws and toss it back into the water. It was the kind of afternoon that should go down in infamy, passed through legend from father to son.

By the time either realized how late it had become, the sun was little more than a pink aura staining the thunderheads that rolled over the jagged peaks of the Rockies to the west. Lightning flashed from one blackened belly to the next, strobing the heavily forested foothills with flashes of pale yellow light. Darkness swelled from the eastern horizon and melted to a deep Atlantic blue overhead. Mosquitoes began settling on the still lake where fish leapt up to engulf them and slapped back down with loud *splooshes*.

"We'd better be getting back," Steve called to his brother. "I'll bet Mom and Dad are preparing to wring our necks now as it is."

"One more cast," Brian called back.

From where Steve stood, the cold, murky water lapping at the apex of his kneecaps, he could see Brian nearly twenty feet up the bank through the swatches of cattails. He was so far into the water that only the upper half of his shorts showed. The thought of wading out there…that deep…made Steve uncomfortable, what with Melinda Wright and all. Maybe she and Kyle had just been skinny-dipping in the lake and had waded out a little too far…. Maybe her ankle had gotten raveled in some of those reeds and when the rain had started coming down, she hadn't been able to free herself as the water just kept rising and rising….

The sting of a mosquito's lance roused him from his trance and he slapped at the back of his neck.

Another poker stabbed into his arm. He reflexively swatted it as well.

There was a high-pitched humming sound as another tickled the fine hairs along his right ear.

"Come on, Brian! I'm getting eaten alive!"

"They're just mosquitoes." Brian sloshed through the reeds, kicking up sprays of water as he ascended the slight slope onto the shore. His rod was already in two pieces, his lure hooked to the side of his creel.

Thunder grumbled across the sky and rolled down the face of the mountains like an avalanche.

A few droplets of rain violated the serenity of the lake.

Steve held his hands out to his sides and craned his neck back to look up into the coming storm. Those clouds were starting to race in fast now, growing thicker and thicker until they reached straight up into the stratosphere. Lightning flared from somewhere within their black depths.

"Starting to rain," Brian said, walking past Steve on the bank with his eyes to the clouds.

Steve wondered if Melinda had looked to the sky and uttered those same words.

VI

With the roiling storm clouds eclipsing the waning light of day, darkness settled over the swamp. The black shapes of ducks dropped from the sky with their wings set and settled into the marsh for the night with lazy, undulant quacks. Sparrows no longer flocked over the tops of the cattails, but rather worked their way into the heavier cover of the willows. The wind arose with a howl. It raced the cold air from the front that was closing in quickly from the east, tossing the cattails sideways and nearly completely obscuring the path before them. Raindrops assaulted them in wretched gusts and announced themselves with a light patter on the flooded plain.

Brain walked in the lead, chin tucked to his chest, eyes raised to see through the shifting reeds that blew first one way then the next, as though the path itself were dancing with him. His right hand stayed at his side, where it could wedge both the creel and his rod case against his hip, while his left swept arcs in front of him, brushing back the cattails. Steve merely watched his brother's heels splashing up muddy water and kept his face down so that none of the reeds would slap him across the eyes. It was getting harder and harder to clearly define his brother's outline against the descending darkness with each step.

A flash of light blossomed above, trailed several seconds later by thunder, grinding across the sky like a slow-moving jet.

In the suppressed twilight, nothing looked familiar. Steve couldn't tell whether this was the path they had come in on or not. It had taken the sparkle from the lake to guide them through the maze of cattails previously. Now, there was nothing but the shrouded stands of cottonwoods towering over them ahead and the reeds stretching infinitely to either side.

"Shouldn't we be to the bikes already?" Steve whined.

"I would've thought so." Brian paused to swing the rig and creel onto his back. He scanned the horizon above the swaying tips of the cattails. Directly ahead was a large cluster of trees that could have been where they had left their bikes. "Right over there!"

Steve looked up long enough to see his brother point straight ahead, down the disappearing path. Raindrops tapped at the side of his face, and the wind drew them in lines across his forehead, plastering down his bangs in clumps. His back was starting to ache with the weight of his rod, forcing him to drag his feet through the flattened reeds, which occasionally snagged a toe and caused him to stumble forward into Brian's back.

He slapped his cheek the moment he felt the sharp tip of a stinger slide into his skin.

Brian did the same. Smacking first at his left ear, then at his back. He brushed the flattened exoskeleton away with a smudge of blood.

It was as though a cloud of mosquitoes had settled over them. The humming was distinctly audible, even over the intensifying scream of the wind.

Lightning shredded the night from behind, followed in short measure by a clap of thunder that sounded like boulders slamming together.

As if on cue, the sky let slip the wrath of the storm. Both boys were immediately soaked through and their clothes clung to them. Steve had to open his mouth to breathe through the sheer volume of water that drained down his face and over his nose. Brian was already dashing toward the tree line, showers of water flying up from his clapping heels.

"Wait up!" Steve cried, breaking into a sprint.

Ahead, the drooping limbs of a willow swallowed the path like the mouth of a basset hound. Cottonwoods older than the swamp itself rose from the marsh, straight up into the clouds, as though the ancient branches held them aloft. Brian disappeared into the thicket with a crash of snapping branches and the sound of leathery leaves being torn from their moorings.

Steve closed his eyes, threw his arms up in front of his face, and barreled through, right behind his brother. The metal tube housing his fly rod snagged on something and a branch snared the strap of his creel. Before Steve even felt his feet leave the ground, the spongy earth rose up and smacked him squarely on the back.

"Oww!" he moaned. He rolled onto his right hip to escape the throbbing pain that blossomed in his left buttock. With all of the broken twigs beneath him, it felt as though he had landed on a cactus.

"Are you all right?" Brian crouched close to Steve's face, though neither could immediately see more than the vague outline of the other's silhouette in the darkness.

Brian slapped the insect crawling on his cheek.

"I think so." Steve managed to finally bring himself to standing with the sound of snapping wood. He brushed what felt like a mixture of mud and moss from his rear end, then swatted at his leg and smeared the biological remains of the bug down toward his knee.

It was as though they had run through the mouth of a cave. Only the most ambitious rays of light arched through the canopy. The branches above sealed out even the pounding rain that had arisen with the wind, now all but a memory outside their sudden haven. They could still hear it, though: gusting sheets of rain hammering the upper reaches of the cottonwoods. The wind still screamed from all around them, but what passed through the dense willows packed between the monstrous trunks of the cottonwoods could barely qualify as a draft.

Brian rose again and slapped first his biceps, then his neck. It sounded like he had a living skin of mosquitoes crawling all over him. The buzzing was like standing beneath high-voltage wires. There was a faint vertical line formed by the side of one of the massive trunks in front of them. It was so wide that it would have taken both of them to wrap their arms around its girth. Steve heard the crackle of dry bark as Brian slid his fingers into the deep trenches between sections. Thin, skeletal branches snapped easily away and fell to the ground.

"I can't see the path anymore," Steve whispered.

"Neither can I."

There was something about the stillness contained beneath the low canopy that inspired a feeling that could almost qualify as reverence.

The branches above snaked together like interlaced fingers, forming a sort of primitive roof. Where they rubbed together, wounds had opened up through the deteriorating bark and sap bled stickily to the ground where it hardened to amber.

Steve smacked both cheeks before immediately curling his fingers to claws and scratching fervently through his hair.

"They're all over me, Brian! Let's just get—"

Lightning flashed through the cove of leaves like fire eating through a wall.

"Shh!" Brian hissed. He knit his brow and craned his head.

Pale yellow light stained the air around them as though from an old fashioned flash bulb. In that stilled moment, the boys could see the thick trunks surrounding them, which cast long shadows back across the ground. The air was thick with clouds of insects, frozen in that instant like smoke.

Steve saw an impression of his brother's face, eyes lowered to the ground, ear cocked warily toward the canopy.

There was a sound. It was hard to describe, but in that moment it had sounded like...like windchimes. But rather than being made from some sort of metal that clanged like church bells, they made the sound of sticks clattering together, like the skeletal rattling of—

Steve sniffed. Something repulsive lingered beneath the scent of decomposing forest and rot. For a second there, he almost thought he smelled raw meat.

Then the lightning was snuffed, and they were smothered by darkness again.

Thunder pounded the earth like the hammer of God.

The lingering residue of the flare of light stained his vision, obscuring whatever detail he may have otherwise been able to decipher from the pitch black.

"Did you see that?" Brian whispered.

He wasn't even sure that *he* had.

"No, what?"

Brian closed his eyes and tried to cling to that dissipating spectre of an image. He had heard that sound and looked up. He had seen a viscous fluid stretching toward the ground. A globule had swelled with gravity, then fallen gently away from the trailing strand of fluid, before finally snapping free. His eyes had followed it, watching that bulbous gob of tackiness slap to the ground. But it hadn't alighted on a mat of fragmented twigs and snapped branches, but rather what looked, in that frozen microcosm of time, to be—

"Bones."

"What?"

"Couldn't have been," Brian whispered, fighting to maintain his grasp on the fleeting picture that slipped through his grasp like mist.

He crouched, careful not to press his bare knees onto the ground. Flattening his right palm, he caressed the earth. It felt like he sifted through nothing more exotic than chunks of bark and jaggedly snapped sections of wood.

He felt the slight weight of insect legs crawling across the back of his neck, the sting of anticoagulants thrust beneath his skin.

Lightning flashed again and Brian saw the ground. Mixed in with the detritus was a scattering of yellowish-brown bone. Cracked teeth, rounded carpals and irregular tarsals, and fractured segments of bone so thin there was no way they had come from anything larger than a bird – all were spread across the sparse dirt and moss.

Steve gasped.

Brian jerked his gaze up, catching first his brother's eyes, and then following their stare up into the canopy.

The debris fell from his hand.

He heard his rod slide off his shoulder and clatter to the ground.

Darkness swallowed the light again, and was immediately chased by a clap of thunder so loud that it startled the mosquitoes from his skin.

He looked to where he knew his brother to be in the absolute darkness, searching for the source of the screaming. Leaping to his feet, he clapped his hand over Steve's mouth and pressed his opposite hand against the base of his brother's skull. But it wasn't until he could feel his brother's closed lips against his clammy skin that he realized the screams were coming from his own mouth as well.

VII

Lightning exploded again, this time no more than a heartbeat ahead of the thunder.

Brian wished he could close his eyes, but for the

life of him, he couldn't steal his stare back from the branches above.

He had never imagined such carnage. How in the name of God had the police not torn this down? Was it possible they hadn't seen it?

There were a good half-dozen squirrels…just common gray squirrels…. They were suspended above him, inverted, and nailed to the wood straight through their fluffy white tails. Fresh sap bled over the rust-flaking nails, which had been pounded until the nail had bent sideways. Stiff arms framed skulls that had been squashed as though beneath a heel: jaws flattened with fractured rodent teeth set askew, swollen tongues protruding through the sides of mouths sealed with congealing blood. They had been slit from jaw to vent, the fur peeled back to expose gooey adipose clusters like so many silver bubbles. Blood drained from their snouts and fell all the way to the ground, where it collected in deep bowls made from the raggedly cropped craniums of what appeared to be bulls, staked into the ground by their savagely broken horns.

A large mammalian leg that appeared to be human swung in the higher reaches, by a rope made from twisted reeds. The violated flesh was severed in tatters where it would have connected to a hip. The meat of the thigh was gnawed in pinkish craters all the way back to the bone. The muscle of the calf was pocked with bites torn from the meat, the edges of the lacerations curled back and crusted.

There were hundreds of other bones somehow staked to those trees. A rodent skull twirled on a length of fishing line, a barbed hook looped through the eye sockets. A large section of the lower lumbar spine and sacrum of what could only have been a deer or an elk hung over space. Ragged sections of dried tissue and fur had been stripped from the vertebrae with the remains of a white-bobbed tail. Bleached bones still bearing rings of fur and hooves were staked to the wood with spikes. A pair of rabbit's feet overlapped against one of the trunks where they had been driven through by a single nail, the cleaned bones dangling down to a severed neck. There were fanned bird wings, as though the creature had been crucified and the meat stolen from between the now dried feathers. A tangle of blood-crusted blonde hair capped a sharpened branch like an avian nest.

Mosquitoes coated the festering meat like a brownish, seething skin, filling nearly every available inch of air space in buzzing swarms.

There was a scrabbling sound from the invisible expanses of branches above, which dropped a shower of bark onto their heads.

The light died, stranding them in a darkness so complete it felt as though a fist had closed around them.

"Go! Go!" Brian screamed. He grabbed Steve by the wrist and jerking him to motion.

Steve stumbled forward, trying to maintain his balance on numb legs. Before he knew it, Brian was dragging him through a mess of foliage that lacerated his face and arms, and tore at his clothing.

His creel snagged, but he just ducked his head, shed it like a reptilian skin, and lost his rig in the process.

Brian's grip on his hand was so tight, so painful, that Steve could only focus on his crumpled fingers, the feeling of the bones grinding together, and allow himself to be led through the mess of limp willow branches and leaves. They charged back into the storm, which welcomed them with a barrage of raindrops and a battering-ram of wind.

VIII

Brian had no idea in which direction he was running. There was no path, only masses of cattails through which he barreled headlong. Foul smelling water splashed up all around him, as though it were raining both from above and below. His ragged breath burst in irregular, rasping gasps. The rain drained through his hair, overflowing his eyebrows and overwhelming his blinking eyelids. It streamed over his lips and into his mouth. He expelled it as a mist with each panicked exhalation.

Steve's cold little hand in his grasp was the only thing binding him to reality.

Everything looked the same. Dense clumps of reeds were packed all around him, betraying only spotted glimpses of the black water beneath on the flooded plain. With a flash, lightning turned night to day in the marsh. Brian shot a glance over his shoulder. Beyond Steve's frightened face, the cattails behind them were flying into the air in tatters, as though ripped from the ground by a tornado.

Brian spun back around again and urged his tired legs to run even faster. He hurdled bowed stands of cattails and swatted the swaying tips back from his face as he charged through. He squeezed Steve's fingers in his fist and tugged his brother with all of his might.

With a ferocious grumble of thunder, the light drained from the sky, leaving them with the fleeting, forked afterglow from the water filling the swamp. It held back the darkness for but a fraction of a second before the enraged night raced in from all sides.

"Come on!" Brian shouted, giving Steve's hand a solid jerk.

"It's right behind me!" Steve screamed.

Brian looked back over his shoulder, but all he could see was the oppressive darkness being beaten back down to the earth by the assault of raindrops.

They crashed forward, tearing reeds from the soft muck by their roots and bending them awkwardly, before stumbling through tangles that looped around their ankles.

A blast of light ignited the sky at the very instant a crash of thunder exploded all around them. Brian turned again, only this time he could see the figure shredding through the cattails behind them. Tatters of weathered black fabric flagged from the outlined head like striking snakes from a gorgon's skull. Where the face should have been was a deep pool of blackness. A clawed hand rose up against the flaring sky and then sliced through the rain, sending severed reeds flying into the swamp.

Those slashing arms appeared no more than inches from the back of Steve's head.

With a scream of terror, Brian threw himself forward, pulling so hard on Steve's arm that he cleaved the smaller boy from his feet. Brian landed on his side and rolled to his back before Steve's weight came down on his chest and knocked the wind out of him.

He wrapped one arm around his younger brother and threw the other up over his face to ward off the attack.

The lightning snapped off like an overhead light between his fanned fingers as the trailing edge of thunder echoed into oblivion.

He screamed again and pinched his eyes tightly shut in preparation for the impact and flailing claws.

His cry shivered on indefinitely, until it eventually died and he had to draw another breath.

Steve trembled against his chest.

Opening his eyes, Brian looked up, fully expecting to see whatever had been in pursuit now looming over him.

But there was nothing.

Nothing but rain coming down from the roiling bellies of the angry, dark clouds above.

"Where'd it go?" he whispered.

He glanced back and forth from left to right and tried to peel apart the layered darkness that had settled all around the sharpened spears of cattails raised against the storm. The reeds beyond his sprawled legs, over his brother's heaving back, still swayed violently from their recent passage.

Nothing.

The rain pattered the standing water all around them, the droplets now so large they felt like pebbles cast from the heavens.

"It was just there…"

Electricity stabbed from the sky, striking the upper reaches of a towering cottonwood, which snapped back and forth as though trying to jerk free. The pulp exploded with a resounding crack, and sent the upper third of the tree crashing through the lower canopy, to splash down in the weeds.

Neither boy heard the sound, as the moment the light flashed from the sky, both could clearly see the figure, towering over them where a moment prior there had been absolutely nothing but statically charged air.

Twin forks of lightning reflected from eyes recessed within a pit of darkness, beneath its tattered cowl.

Grabbing Steve by the shirt, Brian rolled to the side and sprung to his feet, dragging Steve along behind him until he felt his brother gain his legs beneath him with a lurch.

"Go!" Brian wailed, shoving his brother ahead of him and through a wall of cattails.

Steve splashed down into a rising stream and fell to his knees in the muddy bed.

Brian hauled him to his feet by the back of his drenched shirt. Steve coughed up a mouthful of filth-riddled swamp water and gasped for air.

That was when Brian had seen the rusted edges of the circular culvert beneath the road.

"Get in there!" he said, driving Steve right back down to all fours in the stream.

"What about you?"

"Hurry!" Brian pressed his knee into Steve's face to back him toward the pipe.

Steve splashed back to his feet.

Brian latched both hands roughly onto the sides of his younger brother's face.

"You do what I tell you!" Brian snapped. Steve's eyes filled with tears. "You have to hide!"

"Brian…" Steve sobbed.

"I'll find help! You just hide!"

"But—"

"Hurry, or it will see you!"

Brian forced Steve to his knees in the rapidly flowing water.

"Not without you!" Steve screamed, but Brian already had both palms pressed to his face and was shoving him into the darkness and rushing water of the drainage pipe.

IX

How long had it been? Five minutes? Fifteen?

The corrugated ribs of the rusting metal tube pressed so roughly into his shoulders that it felt like teeth slowly sinking into his flesh. He was shivering so badly that he could no longer even hold his hand over his mouth to silence his breathing, which allowed clouds of exhaust to seep out before being ripped from the pipe by the wind.

"B–Br–Brian," he sputtered. He pinched his eyes shut and prayed for his brother to return.

Gravel ground above. Pebbles scuttled down the embankment and plunked into the water outside the pipe. A pair of feet splashed down into the now thigh deep water, and before he could even gasp, fists twisted into his shirt. Fingernails sunk into his skin, and then he was being jerked out of the tunnel and into the storm.

"This road leads to the dairy," Brian said. He had to close his eyes against the siege of raindrops. Lines of water trailed down his face. "I could see the lights."

"How far?" Steve sobbed.

"Half a mile, maybe. Just around that bend." He pointed off down the road, to where three towers of cottonwoods spiraled into the gut of the storm. "Come on!"

Lightning ripped the sky in half, tearing through the tapestry of night.

Brian turned to run back up the steep embankment. A second later, Steve felt warmth splash across his face, forcing him to close his eyes. It stung beneath his eyelids, but he forced them open and saw the jaggedly serrated end of a rusted length of metal protruding from beneath Brian's right clavicle. His older brother pawed at it, his sloppy fingers sliding from the blood-slickened surface.

Steve's eyes locked onto his brother's.

Brian had barely opened his mouth to scream when four clawed fingers clamped over the top of his head, like serpentine fangs. The thin skin tore and sprayed blood. With the clatter of nails against the exposed frontal bone, the figure threw Brian onto his back with an enormous splash. Through the rising water, Steve could see his brother struggling to get to his feet. Brian tried to pry the fingers out of his forehead, but his assailant's grip was too strong. It drove its thumb through the vertex of Brian's skull and started to drag him away like a bowling ball.

"Brian!" Steve screamed.

He lunged out of the culvert and grabbed for his brother's shoes, but they were ripped from his grasp by a figure that appeared to be wearing a cloak formed from darkness itself, which snapped and flagged in decrepit tatters.

Steve coughed out the vile swamp water and drew an inhalation that sounded like a scream.

The figure yanked Brian up from the mire and stomped forward into a line of cattails.

The sky resealed itself, swallowing the lightning with a rumble of thunder.

Steve ran forward, kicking sprays of water up before his knees. Tossing aside the swishing reeds, he hurled himself through and grasped for anything at all.

There was nothing but darkness now, a smothering entity that wrapped around him.

"Brian!"

Lightning flashed again. All he could see were the shivering lances of the reeds, which wavered ferociously from side to side at the behest of the gusting wind.

He spun in a circle, but there was only an endless sea of cattails.

Steve staggered forward and fell to his knees with a loud splash. His head lolled back on his neck. Raindrops pooled in the sockets over his closed eyes and filled his mouth through his parted lips. His arms fell limply to his sides in the marsh.

He let out a pitiful sob that caused his shoulders to begin to shudder.

Brian's blood swirled atop the stagnant water like a skein of oil, encircling Steve's forearms and riding up his thighs.

X

As he sat there on the shoulder of the dirt road, arms wrapped around his knees, Steve thought for a moment that he could understand why Kyle Weatherly had sprayed fiery steel through his forehead.

It had been three days now.

He had watched his mother and father combing through the all-but-impregnable reeds with the police and their bloodhounds, day after never-ending day. He could barely see that gray raft out on the lake from this vantage point. The divers were sitting on the sides with their scuba tanks on their backs. He could tell from their body language and the increasing lengths of inactivity that neither of them really felt that returning to the bottom would accomplish anything.

The flash flood had taken him.

That was the prevailing theory.

Flash flood.

No one believed Steve. Not even his parents.

They hadn't found Melinda. They weren't going to find Brian either.

He rose to his feet on numb legs and stumbled into a skid down the embankment. Small clouds of dust rose from beneath his heels. Gravel tumbled before him into the standing water amidst the cattails. He hopped over a small pool and into the reeds.

This was the first time he had ventured back into the swamp since that night. Consciously, he wasn't precisely sure where his legs were taking him, but there was a small part of him that just had to know…

His memory of that night was foggy. After that thing had taken his brother, Steve recalled the events only in flashes. He remembered the warmth of his brother's blood circulating in swirls atop the otherwise frigid water, the sensation of it caressing his skin. Then he had looked to the heavens, to the flaring underbellies of the dark storm clouds…

He remembered stumbling aimlessly through the cattails—though for how long there was no actual way of knowing. His trembling legs had betrayed him countless times, collapsing beneath him and dropping him to all fours in the frigid mire, leaving him to crawl through the tangled and knotted reeds.

His parents had seen a flash of metal reflecting in the Suburban's headlights as they passed where the boys had hidden their bikes beside the road. They had driven those dirty country roads for hours before winding back toward the lake. Not long afterward, they found Steve stumbling along the side of the road. His knees had been skinned from the top of the patella all the way down to the middle of his shins. Mud coated those nasty wounds like brown scabs. It had been thick in his hair and covered his face to the point that his eyes looked like hollow white orbs, golf balls stamped into the muck. Tears had eroded thin lines through his earthen mask. His shirt had been sapped to him, his shivering arms wrapped around his chest to preserve what little warmth remained. They had wrapped him in the blanket they kept in the trunk, and then everything had turned black.

Steve shifted his awareness back to the here and now.

His legs prickled uncomfortably with goosebumps. Muddy swamp-water, alive with larvae, soaked into his skin all the way up past his knees. Diluted mud covered his hands and forearms to his elbows from falling and shoving himself back to his feet. He could feel the spotted clumps of mud tightening against his cheeks.

Cattails formed a trench around of him, as though he had made his way through the marsh to a path.

A cluster of trees loomed ahead. Formidable cottonwoods reached so high up into the atmosphere that they appeared to be propping up the wispy white clouds. The upper canopy shimmered with the sunlight that reflected from the wide, leathery leaves, the tips of which swayed gently at the urging of a wind that wasn't even strong enough to make its way down to where Steve stood. Willows filled the gaps between the monstrous cottonwood trunks, their swooping branches like cascading water draining from the most placid waterfalls imaginable.

Steve's legs guided him forward once more, guiding him toward the stand of vegetation until he was close enough to reach out and part a pathway through the willows. One step at a time, he eased through the trees. The sharp branches snagged at his shirt and shorts, even his bare flesh, and drew ragged white scratches across his skin. He closed his eyes and didn't open them until he stepped from the clutches of the eager willows into the small clearing beyond.

It felt different in there, as though the air had taken on both a different texture and weight. And he could taste something...like he was sucking on a penny. Finally, he opened his eyes and attempted to rationalize the darkness. Slowly, his vision began to draw contrast from the thin lines of light that filtered from the midday sun through the shivering leaves way up in the highest reaches of the trees, drawing slanting lines to the ground. Infinitesimal motes glimmered like pixie dust in those wan rays of light. The carpet of needles and fractured limbs crackled beneath his shifting weight. He knelt, and sifted through the detritus, allowing the earth to slide between his fingers until he was left with small clusters of bark and snapped twigs, and a triangular, smooth, polished stone. There was a small hole near the base where it had been drilled to accommodate a length of leather.

He rose without dusting himself off and stared up into the lower reaches of the trees above him. Barren branches curled and tangled together like warring vines. The bark had been scraped away to reveal the gray hardwood. They were rich with sap, which blossomed from a multitude of holes and dripped in viscous strands down to the ground, where it accumulated in crusted pyramids like miniature stalagmites.

He recognized this place…only everything was different than it had been.

Steve reached up and touched one of the sappy wounds that appeared to have been inflicted by a nail, and recoiled quickly. At first he hadn't seen them, not with what little sunlight graced the air in that silent cove, and maybe he never would have had he not touched the branch…. But now that he had… now that he knew what he was looking for, it was impossible to overlook.

Mosquitoes formed a living sheath over the wood, climbing all over one another. They were packed so tightly together that one was indistinguishable from the next. There was no buzzing sound or even a single insect in the air. They just coated the trees like a sentient skin.

Mosquitoes.

XI

Steve cast one last glance out the rear window as his father backed the Suburban and the U-Haul trailer attached to its rested hitch out of the driveway.

He watched the garage close for the final time on the emptiness contained within. The window of the bedroom he and Brian had shared stared vacantly at him. He'd never noticed that so many shingles were missing from the roof or how the white paint was peeling away from the red trim. The driveway was cracked, and ambitious weeds grew right up through the seams. The front lawn was more dirt than grass.

He could almost see it shudder a final breath as his father jerked the grinding gears into first and the truck started to roll forward.

Steve looked away from the window and down into his lap, where his hands were neatly folded together with Brian's Indian arrowhead pressed between his palms.

CHAPTER 2

SIXTEEN YEARS LATER

I

A sleek black Cadillac Catera rolled slowly down the dirt lane, the early afternoon sun glinting from the silver trim. A rapidly dissipating rooster tail of dust swelled from behind the rear tires, their tread bearing the brick-red residue of the freshly turned earth. To either side of the road, muddy yellow earth-moving machines stood sentry over tremendous holes in the ground. Stacks of corded two-by-fours were heaped to the left side of each future basement; to the right the enormous mounds of dirt newly carved from the ground. For Sale signs stood where front walks would one day lead to porches, most of them already bearing the bold-lettered "SOLD!" or "Under Contract" placards on top.

The first phase of residential development had sold out within a week of releasing the plots of land. Half of those houses already had residents, and the other half would be fully finished by no later than the end of the following month. That was twenty-two houses in total. Garnet Construction had broken ground on Phase II two weeks prior and was right on schedule.

At least until Stan Garnet received the phone call at precisely 1:43 that afternoon.

His clenched fists wrung the leather wheel of the Catera, his knuckles so white with strain that they looked like snow-capped mountain ranges against the gravel road. His jaw muscles bulged in time with his grinding teeth. Each exhalation came with a grunting sigh, and it felt as though every drop of his stomach acid was eating its way through the entire works of plumbing, from his esophagus straight through to his colon. The chalky residue of half a dozen Maalox tablets still released that foul metallic taste from the crevices of his teeth.

How much was this going to end up costing him? Fifty? A hundred grand?

It was going to take a miracle to keep this place from turning into a three-ring circus by nightfall.

Shaking his head, he watched the wooden signs staked in front of the lots, spray-painted with orange address numbers. 2400. 2410. 2420.

He gently eased the brake down to the floor and coasted to a halt in front of the sign labeled 2430. For the life of him, he couldn't force his ferocious grip to abate from the steering wheel. So he sat there, looking straight ahead through the front windshield at the end of the cul-de-sac. The city had installed the fire hydrant like they had promised. That was something, anyway. And the concrete guys were already pouring the cement footers. Soon they'd have the foundations laid and from there everything was back within his complete control. Jim Savage was the best foreman in the city. Heck, the entire state for that matter. When Jim committed to having a house done on time, Stan could go ahead and confirm the closing date months in advance. Jim never called and whined about lumber prices. Never griped and moaned about his crews or having to deal with all those Mexicans who couldn't speak enough English to order at a Taco Bell. Jim was the kind of man that they had all been once upon a time, the kind of man who would work from sunrise to sunset and do the entire job himself if he had no other choice. He had that old-fashioned work ethic that shamed even Stan's own. And that was really saying something.

With a sigh that highlighted every acid-seething wound throughout his digestive tract, Stan pried his fingers from the steering wheel and threw open the door.

He slipped his Italian loafers from the immaculate floorboards out onto the dirty road and grimaced at not having had the foresight to stick that extra pair of shoes in the trunk for just such an occasion.

Jim never called. In the eight years that Jim had been his foreman, on more jobs than he could count, Jim had never called him to say anything but that the job was complete.

Unbuttoning his charcoal suit jacket, Stan ran

his right hand roughly over his mouth, ruffling his thick, gray-peppered black mustache that back in the day had made him look like Tom Selleck. His lips writhed angrily against one another. He closed his eyes momentarily, just long enough to summon the strength he was going to need.

He walked around the front of the car, shoving his keys into his pants pocket, and strode directly down the long drive toward the hole in the ground.

It looked as though the entire crew was crowded around the pit, staring down curiously, holding their hard hats beneath their arms like footballs, dragging the beading sweat from their brows with the backs of their forearms. Every white T-shirt was stained in various unappealing patterns, though the majority stood there bare-chested, the dirt turning to mud against their damp, brown skin. Past them he could see the rows of cottonwoods lining the northern bank of the lake and the faint glimmer of the sun on the distant water. Leveled dirt led right to the edge of the marsh, where yellow and brown cattails were crumpled over beside their exposed roots.

The hint of sulfur lingered in the air like flatus.

As soon as the men saw him coming, they began to drift away like flies startled from a corpse.

Stan stormed right up to the edge of the cut and stared down into the hole.

"Are you sure they're real?" he asked.

Jim tipped the brim of his dusty hard hat back and looked up from where he crouched on the ground, faded jeans rife with swatches of dirt from swiping his gloved hands. He closed his right eye against the sun and scratched at his scruffy cheek with the back of his grungy fist.

"Would I have called you if they weren't?" Jim asked, rising to his feet. He sauntered over to the slanted edge of the foundation, where the dirt was still kept at an angle to allow them to drive the tractors down.

Stan was already halfway down the embankment, the soft earth absorbing his expensive shoes all the way up past his ankles, where the loose dirt rode up over the tops of his socks and against his bare legs.

"No," Stan said, lowering his voice. He looked anxiously up from beneath his brow at Jim. "I don't suppose you would have."

Jim nodded his sun-leathered face, his azure eyes framed by crow's feet and lines worn deeper by the constant exposure to the sun's rays and sandpaper wind.

"Where did you find them?" Stan asked, now in a whisper barely loud enough for Jim to hear over the slight breeze.

"Rico found them right down there," Jim said, heading toward the far end of the rectangular hole where a portion of the flattened dirt wall had collapsed into a pile of debris. "Said he accidentally clipped that wall there with the tip of the tractor's plow while trying to move some of the dirt back out, and that section just fell down."

Stan appraised the mound of dirt. There appeared to be nothing out of the ordinary.

"At first he thought it was just a network of roots. You know how these cottonwood runners are everywhere in the ground around here. He said he thought it looked odd, so he hopped down to take a look. I think he knew he messed up and was trying to figure out a way to get that wall of dirt smoothed back into place before anyone found out."

Stan walked right up to the edge of the heaped terra and crouched before it. He shoved back his coat sleeves and took a moment to unbutton his cuffs and roll them carefully to his elbows. With a snap, he unfastened the clasp on his platinum Rolex, folded it neatly in half and inserted it into his pocket.

"They aren't down there in the dirt, if that's what you're thinking," Jim said before Stan could shove his manicured nails down into the pile.

"Then where…?" Stan started, but the words died the moment he raised his head.

"Right there," Jim said, taking a step back.

Jim obviously couldn't stand being so close to them, as though he could somehow be connected to them through proximity. But it wasn't just that, it was the way they looked. It was just…. The only word that could really do what he was seeing any kind of justice was "tortured."

"My God," Stan gasped, clapping his hand over his mouth.

II

Stan toppled back onto his rear end, still holding his hand over his mouth despite the streak of dirt that now marred his slacks. His hazel eyes snapped so wide open that the lashes disappeared into the creases. The irises trembled back and forth.

He scuttled backwards, kicking at the earth.

Stan didn't know exactly what he had expected to find, but this was certainly not it.

Packed into the wall as though tramped beneath God's tread was an arrangement of yellowish-brown bones, highlighted by the crusted dirt packed into the fine crevices. The soil surrounding the skeleton was rich and black, like the kind of potting soil landscapers used. There was the distinct framing of a ribcage stuffed with dirt like a turkey. A lone disjointed humerus led away from a severely fractured clavicle. Above, a skull stared directly at him through eye sockets packed with dirt. A lightning bolt fracture bisected the frontal bone. The mouth was contorted into a wide, eternally-fixated scream, the lower jaw set askew to the left. Manila teeth spotted the compressed dirt between like kernels of corn.

To the left, there was the rounded bowl of the base of a cranium, the suture wrenched wide like a Muppet's mouth. Jaggedly fractured cervical vertebrae trailed away from it like a tail, the spinous processes haphazardly snapped off. The angled joints between segments were torqued so badly that rather than lining up nicely, facet to facet, they appeared more like stairs. Twin triangular shoulder blades were set to either side of what remained of the thoracic spine, between which all of the posterior ribs had been roughly severed. The knobbed ends of the distal portion of the femora poked through the dirt above the head as though the body had been forcefully balled and shoved down a shallow chute.

Dozens of other loose bones in no apparent pattern or formation pocked the firm earth, ranging in size from fragments no larger than pebbles to a random bone that appeared too thick to have come out of a human body.

"Oh God," Stan moaned, wrenching his hand from his mouth and turning away.

From the way those bodies were twisted and contorted, the way the one face was stilled in an eternal scream of agony, Stan could tell that whoever they were, they had died badly.

"What do you want me to do with them?" Jim asked. He looked directly into Stan's eyes.

Stan glanced back at the wall of bones, closed his eyes, and turned back to Jim.

"I said…what would you like me to do with them?" There was no emotion in Jim's face, just the stoic indifference of a man who might just as easily have been asking about the weather forecast.

"What do you mean?" Stan asked, clearing his throat and adjusting his red satin tie. He forced himself to his feet, swayed, and began the seemingly insurmountable task of regaining his composure.

"I mean, where did we find the bones?"

"I don't understand." Stan winced like he'd been punched in the gut and gingerly placed his hand on the left side of his abdomen. Sudden onset of an ulcer, he suspected.

"If we uncovered these bones right here, within the foundation of this lot, then this would become a crime scene. If the police were to assume authority over this area, we could easily lose two or three weeks. Not to mention the negative publicity that would surround the entire Kettner Lake development."

"I know," Stan said, finally securing his wits again. "The financial implications are staggering, but what alternative do we have?"

"They could turn up somewhere else," Jim said. He rubbed at the back of his neck where the sun had baked the flesh red. "Or they could never turn up at all."

"Like where?"

Jim crossed his arms over his barrel chest. A thin smile slowly parted his cracked lips.

CHAPTER 3

THE SHALLOWS

I

From her vantage, the lake appeared to be on fire as it reflected the awesome display of oranges and reds of the sun, which was setting contentedly behind the cresting Rockies behind her. The small waves shimmered like flickering flames through the needle-tipped reeds. Somewhere out there in the marsh, a pair of geese honked dreamily back and forth, their droning tone drifting into the night sky.

This was Teri's favorite time of day. The time when the cackling starlings retreated into their nests to bed down for the night, when the ducks prepared to tuck their bills beneath their wings, when the deer foraged through the last of the waning light before folding their legs beneath them in the high grasses. This was that magical hour when the golden hue of the dwindling sun was replaced by the halogen aura of street lamps, when leather-winged creatures flapped madly against the darkness, darting swiftly through the groups of moths that battered at the artificial lights. This was the time when twilight crept in from the horizon and tucked the world beneath a blanket of night like a sleeping child.

Some great distance away, the faint whistle of a train haunted the swamp.

Teri closed her eyes and allowed the cool breeze to gently caress her face and sift through her bangs like magical fingers. Her long chestnut hair, streaked with blonde highlights as though weaved in by an artist's brush, trailed over her shoulders to the middle of her back. She couldn't help the blissful smile that slowly spread across her lips. When she finally opened her aquamarine eyes, the canvas of the twilight had been washed clean of all but the subtlest shades of blue and gray.

In that moment, she was at peace with everything around her. Between the lingering din of the parting day and the encroaching night, she felt as though she had been granted a momentary reprieve from all her troubles.

"Come on, Bo," she whispered, unable to find her voice through the almost euphoric feeling that consumed her.

With a jangle of the tags on his collar, the chocolate lab rose from his haunches and tested the length of the red leash. His olive green eyes scanned the shifting reeds for the first sign of something to chase.

Teri paused long enough to scratch behind those floppy brown ears, then started forward from the shoulder of the dirt road, toward the thin path that disappeared into the swishing cattails.

Bo tugged ahead as much as he knew she could tolerate. He lowered his snout to the ground and sniffed frenetically in every direction. There hadn't been a single night on one of their walks that he hadn't flushed some sort of waterfowl or chased a squirrel or rabbit from the thicket. This was his territory now, and every fifteen yards he hitched a leg and marked it as such.

Teri had been one of the first to move into the development when they had opened it. She had lucked into the deal before the value of the land had escalated astronomically. The money for the down payment had come from the trust fund her parents had left her, the remainder of which was enough so that if she managed everything properly, she ought to still be able to earn enough in interest to pay the mortgage without dipping into the principle. Granted, she would have rather her mother hadn't succumbed to breast cancer and that her father hadn't chased her to the grave in a self-destructive assault on his liver, but aside from that, for the first time in as long as she could remember, things were starting to work out.

After graduating *summa cum laude* from the University of Colorado's School of Engineering with an emphasis in theoretical physics, the job offers hadn't come pouring in as she had hoped. The U was already fully staffed, and résumé after résumé found that every other graduate school in the state was overstocked in the physics and engineering departments, but suggested that she might find teaching high school physics to her liking. She could only imagine turning her back to lecture to a group of post-pubescent boys, all of whose eyes would undoubtedly fall directly on her posterior. The prospect was about as appealing as an elective colonoscopy; somehow she managed to resist the urge.

It took close to six months after graduation to finally land not just any old job, but the job that appeared to be the foot in the door to her dreams. The pay was less insulting than it was humbling, but the job itself was what she had been grooming herself for since the first time she sat under an apple tree, waiting for Newton's Law to rear its ugly head.

Theoretical physics was what they called "soft" science, meaning that there were no immediate means of either testing or proving their hypotheses. They dealt in theory, though not in the same context generally ascribed to philosophy, for which theory was often mistaken. Their data may not have been quantitative, but every theorem owed its foundation to fairly simple mathematical premises. She worked in research, basically feeding formulae and logarithms into a computer to justify the grant money. So it was grunt work, and it was at a junior college rather than a four-year institution. But they needed their professorship to publish, and she needed the opportunity to do so, to make a name for herself, no matter how small.

Bo stopped in his tracks and allowed the leash to fall slack as she closed the distance. He raised his head up high on his straight neck. His ears gracefully rolled back. One by one, it seemed, the hairs along his nape prickled to match the similar swatches at the base of his spine and along his stiffened tail.

"What is it, boy?"

Bo stood perfectly still. He stared directly ahead through the wavering grasses, which shifted before him like a milling crowd, obscuring his line of sight down the path.

Teri crept up on him, suddenly acutely aware of the dry reeds crunching beneath her feet. She placed her hand on his haunches, into the almost statically charged bristle, and Bo flinched as if she had hit him.

Slowly, deliberately, he lowered his head toward the ground until his eyes were below the level of his shoulders. His entire body trembled as he began to growl.

"It's all right," she whispered.

Bo shot forward so quickly that Teri didn't even have a chance to tighten her grip on the leash. It flew from her hand to the ground and trailed the dog's bounding rear end straight into the reeds, which swallowed him whole. He let loose a terrible barrage of barking as he crashed through the cattails, tearing whole stalks from the ground before his heaving chest.

"Bo!" Teri shouted.

She raised both hands in front of her face to ward off the reeds and sprinted down the path.

II

"Bo!" Teri shouted, stamping through the thick undergrowth. "Come on, boy."

It wasn't like Bo to run off like this. She couldn't think of a time that he had done so since he had been a puppy. Usually when some animal or other darted off into the weeds, he'd plant his rear end down on the ground, look at her with those wide puppy eyes, and emit an anxious whine. She'd generally oblige, so long as there weren't many other people around, and unlatch the leash from his collar to let him thunder off into the reeds. He'd appear again a couple minutes later—at most—usually wet with that pungent swamp-water, mud clear up his haunches and covering his snout from where he had shoved it into whatever burrow the creature had raced down.

Her best guess was that it had been close to ten minutes now.

"Bo! Come!" she shouted and then released a frustrated sigh.

There was a sudden sting on the back of her neck. She slapped at it, and smeared away most of the mosquito with a thin trace of her already-drawn blood.

She rubbed at the itching, swelling growth and cursed beneath her breath.

"Bo!"

Shaking her head, she trudged forward through the maze of cattails. The sun had long since abandoned her, and the remaining blue in the sky was beginning to bruise black. Pinholes of light poked through the tapestry of darkness. The waxing half-moon filtered through the downy swatch of clouds that drifted lazily along the trace breeze.

After several minutes of silence, interrupted by nothing more tangible than the crunch of her footfalls through the night and the sound of small waves lapping at the sandy bank, Bo finally announced himself with a series of loud barks.

"Bo!" she called, darting forward through the tangles of reeds, toward the source of the sound.

The barking continued in earnest, though it had lost its imperative tone.

She blew through a stand of cattails and padded onto the soft bank.

Bo looked back at her over his shoulder, his eyes reflecting the moonlight like twin golden beacons. He let out a single bark, then turned his attention back to the lake and waded in several steps until the water tickled his belly.

He raised his nose and sniffed, tasted the wind, then waded in just a little bit farther.

"Get out of the water!" she snapped. She stomped along the bank until she was even with the spot where he had waded in. Clouds of mud swirled in the water where he had stirred the bed.

Teri reflexively smacked her right arm the moment she felt the pinch of the mosquito bite.

"What the hell?" She swatted her cheek next. "Come on, boy! Time to go!"

Bo turned back to face her and started to whine.

She studied the still lake before her, expecting to

see some sort of large rodent or injured fowl splashing out there in the mirrored darkness, but the only movement came from the circular, rippled patterns of the gently rising water against the stalks of the reeds.

"I don't have time for this, Bo," Teri whined. She strode right up to the edge of the water, the mud squishing over the tops of her tennis shoes. "Come on."

Bo looked back out to the middle of the lake one last time, then turned and trotted through the water toward her. He shoved his nose down into the shallows. Muddy water splashed up over his snout and forced him to close his eyes. Jerking his head back, he shook the water from his fur and pranced right up to her, chomping loudly on what sounded like a thick stick.

"Drop it!" she commanded, but Bo just sidled up beside her and rubbed his wet flank against her right leg.

She reached toward his mouth to excise the stick.

Bo jerked his head back, lowered his haunches, and let out a low, barely audible growl.

"Oh, no. Don't even think you're going to turn on me and growl."

She grabbed him by the collar, gave it a sharp tug, and reached with her free hand into his slobbering mouth. Wrapping her fingers around the branch, she tugged it toward her, and, with a twist, pried it from his jaws.

"We won't be taking these little walks anymore if you aren't going to behave yourself, mister." She turned away from him and prepared to cast the stick off into the weeds, but she knew that would only trigger his "fetch" reflex. She had no choice but to hold onto it until Bo was distracted by something else and try to secretly discard it into the thickest clump of cattails she could find. "What's gotten into you, boy? You've never in your life growled at—"

Her breath caught with a hitch.

She closed her eyes and her face contorted into a knot of concentration. Her right hand caressed the smooth surface of the stick, following the slightly bowed, porcelain-like contour. One end was much thinner than the other and capped with what felt like a knob with a dull point. The other end was thicker, and she was almost sure that it had something resembling a hook on it.

Bo whined for the object in her hands.

A mosquito buzzed so close to her ear that it sounded as though it was in the canal, while another alighted on her left biceps.

"Jesus."

She immediately dropped it and swiped her hands on her jeans.

III

Teri stared down at that thing on the bank in front of her feet. Her right hand was pressed tightly over her open mouth after stifling a gasp. When she realized that she had been holding the bone with that same hand, she hurriedly drew it away.

Bo tried to sneak in and grab it for himself again, but she swatted him on the nose, and he cringed back.

Was it human?

No. No, it couldn't possibly be human. It had to have belonged to a deer or something. The length was about right. Maybe a cow? Too small. A bear? Again, too small.

She looked at Bo's front legs, but the shape was all wrong.

Then she dropped her gaze to her own forearm where she could feel a mosquito sucking her blood.

There was no way she could deny it any longer. She'd taken anatomy. This was one of the most distinct bones in the human body. The ulna. The end of the hook was the olecranon process; the half circle was where the trochlear surface of the medial humeral condyle articulated. The bone tapered toward the distal head, which was capped with a small, blunt styloid process, where the radius and ulna met to form the distal radioulnar joint at the wrist.

She turned her palms up and let the moonlight wash over them.

It positively made her stomach churn. She had held a human bone in her hands—something that had once been inside another living person—yet it had been all by itself in the lake.

Or so she had assumed.

Teri drew her gaze from her hands and to the shallows, where the mud Bo had stirred was nearly completely settled again. The crescent moon shimmered on waves that suddenly felt as though they emanated a bitter chill. Goose bumps rose along the backs of her arms.

She smacked a mosquito on her cheek, then briskly rubbed her eyes.

"Come on," she said softly. She bent over and grabbed the looped handle of the leash, which was saturated with water and mud from being dragged through the marsh.

Bo whined again, and raised his brows.

"No," she said, shaking her head. There was still a clump of gristle on the thin end of the bone, like the knot of tendons atop a drumstick.

With a weak tug, she brought Bo's legs to motion and turned back toward the path that would lead them home.

IV

Teri sat out on the back porch beneath the overhanging roof in a folding lawn chair. The bug zapper hummed from her right where it dangled by a hook from the roof, emanating a surreal blue glow that illuminated the porch like a caged star. Little more than a rectangular patch of leveled dirt, her back yard stretched toward the waiting cattails that stood like the last line of defense against the advance of civilization.

Bo sat beside her, leash wrapped around the support post. He stared patiently toward the swamp. The searchlights reflected in his unblinking eyes.

The bug zapper crackled and snapped as the mosquitoes fried on the parallel tubes beneath the wire mesh.

She had shut off all of the lights in the house behind her so that she could better see what was going on down there by the distant lake, which was little more than a glimmer of moonlit tranquility through the swarming reeds. She could hear their voices, far off, dissipating into the night like ghostly sounds. Occasional words materialized from the ether, but little of any real coherency.

Behind her, restless storm clouds crept stealthily over the Rocky Mountains, grumbling eagerly with thunder. The advancing front brought with it sinus pressure that swelled behind her eyes. Sporadic flashes of lightning strobed the field before her, though only dimly, hardly enough to outline the shapes of the cottonwoods against the stain from the lights of downtown Denver against the eastern horizon.

Flashlights arced across the surface of the lake and sifted through the underbrush, though not with the same zeal with which they had begun.

"I'll bet they found more," Teri whispered. She scratched behind Bo's floppy ears with her left hand. He leaned into the pressure, but still focused his attention on the far-off lake. Every couple of seconds he raised his damp black nose and inhaled the breeze when it shifted. "Otherwise they'd be gone by now."

The police hadn't arrived until quarter to ten, but

hadn't been as initially skeptical as Teri had thought they would be. Judging by their reactions, it was almost as though they had been expecting her call. She knew they couldn't have been, though. She was tired, and certainly not quite in a rational state of mind. She was still reeling from the fact that not so long ago she had been holding a bone that had been beneath the skin of someone who at some point had been a living, breathing human being. The problem was that the whole episode had been out of context. She could have held the exact same bone in a science lab, turning it over and over in her hands, and inspected it from every appreciable angle without thinking anything of it, but down there by the lake… Feeling it in her hands, still grimy from the muck, the fine fissures thick with packed mud, it had felt so…tainted.

Teri yawned. She covered her mouth with a hand that positively stank like detergent from the furious scrubbing, and settled even further into the chair.

She hoped that she had been wrong, that it hadn't been a human bone at all, but rather a coyote's leg or whatnot that some creature had dragged off to gnaw at the lake's edge.

But the police wouldn't still be down there then, would they? They would have walked to the shore, taken a good long look at the bone, chuckled at her stupidity, and then tossed the thing back into the lake so they wouldn't have to try to figure out what to do with it.

The pair of officers who had arrived at her door with the bored expressions and nondescript faces had been down by the lake for close to two hours now, she guessed. The policeman who had held out a notepad and pointed a pen at it as though preparing to take down her story, but had never actually written anything, had promised that if there were anything to be concerned about, he'd make sure to return and let her know. Since then, more and more slants of light had appeared down behind the walls of willows, where she could swear she had heard the sound of tires grinding along the dirt road.

"What did you guys find?" Teri whispered to herself, watching as now close to a dozen sabers of light slashed through the reeds. She brushed innocuously at a mosquito that hummed beside her ear.

A flash of blue light filled the sky from the other side of the house and threw its strobing shadow out across the marsh.

Bo whined and darted for the sliding glass door, jerking to a halt several steps short, at the end of his tether. He sat, looked back over his shoulder at the swamp, and started to shiver.

Thunder grumbled down the mountains and across the plains.

The first raindrops pattered with tiny footsteps on the shingles overhead.

"What did you find?"

CHAPTER 4

PUZZLES

I

It had changed him.

In that one moment, time had stood still and allowed him to engrave the sights, sounds and smells into his memory to forever haunt him. His childhood had been slaughtered and ripped away from him. The course of his life had been irrevocably altered.

He had been thirteen years old when it happened.

Thirteen.

And between the time he laid his head down on the pillow to sleep that night and the time he awoke to the thunderous report, he had aged well beyond his years. In every childhood, the loss of innocence can be traced to a series of events that metamorphose the wonder of naïveté into the grim reality that is the dawning of adolescence. For Kevin Weatherly, it hadn't been a gradual progression that had led to the end of his childhood, but a single, gruesome event that had taken everything he knew about life and hacked it into pieces, never again to be reassembled.

Every detail from that night was fresh and poignant, from the texture of the paper of the *Uncanny X-Men #213* he had been reading before his mother had forced him to turn off the light, to the smell of the roast that had lingered well after it had been fully consumed. He could still feel the soft support of the pillow beneath his head as he stared upward, and watched arcs of light flash across the ceiling from the storm outside. The open door to the darkened hallway had cast a shadow against the wall like a wizard with a pointed hat. And the prevailing image that had welcomed him into slumber's embrace was raven-haired Kelly Hawkins with her shiny new braces and eyes so blue they blazed like the flame of a Bunson burner.

"Have you lost your mind?"

That had been the last thing he had said to Kyle. The last thing he would ever say to his big brother.

He had heard Kyle talking on the phone to his girlfriend using that lovey-dovey little Elmer Fudd voice that he used when telling Melinda how much he loved her. Kevin had leaned through the doorway into his brother's room—where Kyle had been sprawled on his back, holding the phone to his left ear and tossing a football up to the ceiling with his right—and had uttered those last words.

"Have you lost your mind?"

He'd remember those words for the rest of his life, along with the image of Kyle's brains dripping in chunks to the concrete floor of the garage.

II

Kevin bolted upright in his darkened room and tossed the covers off his bare chest. A cold film of sweat clung to his body, and glistened on his face with each flash of lightning. His heart was racing.

11:42 pm, the clock on his dresser stated in large, blood-red numbers.

Something had jarred him sharply to consciousness, like the crack of a bat across the base of his skull. He searched the swirling miasma between the waning dream and his dawning consciousness. The final fading image from the dream was of a head-on car collision. Two metallic bodies slamming into each other with a resounding explosion that sounded like—

His mother's scream pierced the darkness.

—gunfire?

"Oh God!" his father wailed over his thudding footsteps as he sprinted down the hallway. He slammed his shoulder into the wall right next to Kevin's room before he redirected himself toward the stairs and pounded down them to the tune of the groaning railing that strained against its moorings. "Oh please, God!"

"No!" his mother cried, dropping from the bed to the floor with a resounding crash.

"What's going—?" Kevin rasped, but his voice momentarily failed him. "What's going on?"

There was a ringing sound in his ears.

Kevin lowered his legs over the side of the bed in slow motion. The fibers of the carpet squeezed up between his toes. A simple transference of weight, and he was fully upright and creeping through a fugue toward the hallway in nothing but his shorts.

His mother's tortured screams echoed down the hallway from her room, where the last of her frayed sanity was stripped away with the lining of her trachea.

Veering left, Kevin guided himself down the stairs to the landing. His right hand found the iron railing and curled it tightly into his damp palm. The cold radiated up his forearm, as though he had impaled his palm on a sharpened icicle. He descended the staircase, detached, as if watching the scene on a flickering eight-millimeter reel inside the confines of his mind. The lightning shattered the otherwise all-consuming darkness in pale blue flashes from the sliding glass door in the kitchen. His body moved of its own accord, guiding him steadily forward until the soles of his feet transferred from the carpeted staircase to the cold, gray slate tile of the foyer. It felt as though he floated across it, his skin grazing across it as though it were a thin layer of ice.

A crash of thunder beckoned him toward the kitchen, and the stairs leading down into the family room. The entire house vibrated on its foundation beneath the assault of the storm, and when the blue light flared again, he could see rivers of water racing down the glass and, beyond, the tall grove of cottonwoods that swayed violently in defiance of the wind outside.

His body turned left, though by now he was little more than a passenger inside his flesh, an observer surveying the shadows draped across the furniture in the family room as he descended. Darkness slithered like a mist around his feet.

Light angled across the worn beige carpet in front of the entryway to the garage, highlighting the worn tracks and the strands of twine that had peeled back from the unraveling pile.

"Oh, God!" his father moaned. The acoustics of the closed garage amplified not only the guttural sound, but the pain in his father's voice as well. The words positively dripped with tears. Kevin heard a wet slapping sound like a saturated towel flung to the ground. His father wailed again, only this time the words dissolved into sobs that Kevin could feel in the pit of his stomach.

His trembling, stilted legs guided him onward, toward the open door. He watched as his left hand reached out, grabbed the brass handle, and gently pulled it open. The cold cement of the twin stairs greeted his feet as he descended again, into the oppressive air that felt somehow dirty, clogged with dust that wouldn't allow him to breathe freely. His eyes burned from the haze of sulfuric discharge, and at first, it was all he could smell. The hood of the brown Bronco reflected the overhead fluorescent light. Dusty webs filled the corners, where their eight-legged occupants waited patiently within spiraling silk cocoons.

The gunpowder scent mingled with the stink of motor oil and gasoline, and the smell of cooked dust that came from behind the meat freezer against the wall, where butchered carcasses of deer and elk slowly melted through the freezer burn into a frost-covered layer of blood. And overriding it all was the unmistakably vile aroma of rent flesh. It was that first gust of air that exploded past the bloodied hilt of a knife stabbed into the gut of an elk. It was that same odor that rolled like a fog over the eviscerated innards of that carcass. It was the smell of flesh scorched by a bullet and the resultant spout of blood that poured from it like a hastily tapped spigot.

It was the smell of death.

"Please, God!" his father railed. Kevin could hear his old man slamming his fists repeatedly onto the concrete. "Please, God! Don't take him from me! I beg of you! Don't take my son away from me!"

Kevin brushed aside the door to the third garage and floated in. Directly ahead of him was his father's work table, where there were jars of assorted screws and nails, the glass mottled with ugly gray smears from the oils on those small spikes. Sawdust covered the particle-board bench around what appeared to be a chunk of drywall from the ceiling above. The single overhead bulb dangled uselessly by electrical cords and issued a sickly yellow glow that seemed to do little more than make shadows grow from everything in the garage.

To his left was an entire wall of cupboards, but he

didn't even have to look in that direction. His father was kneeling on the floor right in front of him, hunched over a pair of legs that terminated in sloppy brown socks and mud-coated tennis shoes.

A pool of scarlet spread around him on the floor, widening as he watched. It shimmered beneath that awful amber glare.

Kevin closed his eyes and turned away. There was a moment when the darkness behind his lids felt like the welcome embrace of sanctuary, but again his lids parted to reveal the wall in front of him. Fine droplets of blood clung to the surface as though painted on by a mist, while larger droplets dripped toward the floor. Lines of the warm fluid poured like syrup from the ceiling.

His father's cries intensified to the point that they overwhelmed him. His auditory senses shut down, and left him stranded in that putrescent yellow glare with all of the blood and the corpse beneath his father's shuddering form.

The black barrel of the shotgun puffed a wispy ring of smoke that dissipated into a single finger, pointing up to the ceiling.

Kevin was helpless against the urge to follow the ascent of the tendril of smoke to where a ragged black hole had been punched through the ceiling. It was surrounded by countless smaller holes where individual pellets had passed through. His mother's fingers worked through the holes as though trying to reach down to them. Dust still lingered around the shredded drywall, through which he could barely make out a fractured wooden joist supporting the flat plywood slat that was the floor above.

Blood poured from the gash in the ceiling as though the shotgun blast had opened a wound in the house itself, which dripped chunks of gray matter, rife with wrinkled convolutions and sloppy with the warm fluid.

A glob quivered from the ceiling, then shivered loose and dropped to his cheek with a *splat*.

Kevin closed his eyes and felt the remainder of the roast rise in revolt from his stomach, the warmth of the slick trail left by the slimy chunk slithering down his face like the trail of a slug.

His eyes rolled skyward beneath his upper lids, and the black void yawned wide and engulfed him whole.

III

Kevin woke in a cold bath, with his knees pulled up against his chest. The water was murky and pink with the residue of his brother, most of which clung to his skin and knotted at the base of the fine hairs covering his body. He was still wearing his shorts, though the white briefs looked more like they had been tie-dyed with a mosaic of human suffering.

His bony, trembling fingers clattered against his kneecaps, barely above the level of the water that summoned the goose bumps that prickled his flesh and spilled over the sides of the overflowing, grout-stained basin.

His breaths hitched in stolen gasps. The muscles in his face twitched of their own volition, as though with the sudden onset of so many tics. Lines of slobber drained over his bluing lips, connecting his mouth with the wavering surface of the water. His shoulders were hunched up to brace his head and keep it from lilting awkwardly off to the side.

To his right, the small white tiles were separated by grisly brown seams of mildew; the once mirror-smooth surface thickened by grime. Fresh crimson handprints covered the wall where they were already beginning to drain in parallel lines toward the rim of the tub.

Water roared from the nozzle, filling the tub with an icy current that caused his groin to squeeze and constrict. Both of the plastic handles were coated with a layer of blood that obscured the large H and C on the front of each. Spirals of blood from his knuckles encircled them on the tile. In his left ear he could hear the water splashing onto the floor, where it had already formed a substantial puddle that drained like a waterfall down through the slanted grates of the floor vent. It raced musically through the aluminum ductwork.

The faint residue of his crimson footprints dissolved into the spreading water, which now leeched into the carpet in the hallway.

Kevin's entire body shook, and he let out a pained moan that buckled his head back against his shoulders.

He raised his hands to bury his face in his palms, but all of the fine lines were highlighted with a caked layer of dried blood that smudged like oil pastels.

Thrusting them down into the water, he wrung them between his suddenly parted knees until it felt as though he could have peeled the skin right off and shed the whole works like sloppy gloves. He was certain his hands that would never again feel remotely clean.

As his own blood seeped through the self-inflicted fissures in his knuckles, Kevin's head lolled forward and bounced up and down as his shoulders shuddered.

Tears welled over his lower lashes and dropped in swelling globules from the tip of his nose, splashing down into the cold water where his blood diluted with what remained of his brother's.

IV

Kevin hadn't been back to that tract of land in over a decade. Not since his parents had finally sold their old house. They had tried valiantly to live their lives in the face of the tragedy, to let everyone who looked in from the outside know that they were all right, but it had driven his mother from her right mind. She had never been able to bring herself to go back into her own bedroom, where her eldest son's hot blood had exploded through the floor on so many steel pellets, even after they had healed the wound in the floor and completely replaced the carpet in favor of a pristine white that resembled fresh snowfall. She had still insisted that she could see his blood, spattered on the deep pile like so many albino eyes watching her every movement.

She had chosen to sleep on the couch in the family room, angled so that she could see the door to the garage, should Kyle eventually try to return through the same route he had exited. Her ratty blanket had smelled as dour as she had, her hair a mat of tangles that mimicked the contour of the arm of the couch. Beneath she had clutched her "bottles," as they had come to know them. In her right hand had been the little brown vial that held the Valium, which had rattled like a diamondback's tail in her trembling grasp, and in her left, the bottle of vodka she had used to chase those pills down into the empty shell she had become.

His father had busied himself with renovations, often waking Kevin in the middle of the night with the scream of the circular saw or the pounding of nails. In retrospect, he figured his old man had thought that if he could have made the house over into something new, he might have been able to chase away the ghosts that haunted the old. Apparently, all the bay windows and sunrooms in the world couldn't rid him of a fraction of the guilt he had felt. They had moved down to the city just under a year after that horrible night.

Kevin didn't know how he had handled it, or if he even had at all. He treated the memories like a stomach virus, forcing them down as soon as they rose and started to gag him, chasing them away into the darkness that always seemed to be waiting. The sight of his brother's corpse had branded him in a very real way. The image had been burned into the insides of his eyelids, where it would always be waiting for him when he closed his eyes. And even now, so many years later, he often still scratched at his bare arms, thinking he felt the skin tightening with the crust of Kyle's dried blood.

Now, staring through the windshield into the night, he was at the mercy of all of those old feelings…all of the fear and the rage and the terror that he forced into a knot at the center of his being. Three police cruisers were lined side to side against the backdrop of the shadowed trees, which changed colors with the swirling red and blue lights from their roofs. The entrance to the thin path through the willows beckoned like a mouth, opening wide and whispering of promises and secrets before closing gently on the flaccid breeze.

He'd been sitting there for close to half an hour, unable to bring himself to pull the handle on the door and open it into the night. The windshield wipers shivered back and forth, drawing arcs through the raindrops that pattered softly on the glass, refracting the colors of the police cherries. His exhalations clouded the glass before dissolving in slow, concentric circles, until there was nothing left and another breath started the whole process over again.

What was he doing out here anyway? He was a clinical psychologist after all, not some sort of criminologist. He counseled couples contemplating divorce, though he himself lived in an apartment while his ex-wife frolicked with her new beau in the house they had bought together. He went spelunking in the minds of people victimized by erectile dysfunction, agoraphobia, and countless other psychological maladies for which the cure was only a matter of sleight-of-hand, like a magician's trick. They wanted so badly to believe that there was a rabbit in his black top hat that all he needed was to show them a tuft of white fur, and that was good enough. He attempted to talk forlorn and depressed teenagers out of committing suicide—and with reasonable success—though each time he sat in a room with one of those kids and listened to their endless tirades about the mean, cruel world and how no one understood them, all he could see was his older brother nuzzling up to that well-oiled barrel, pinching his eyes shut so tightly that tears squeezed out, and grinding his teeth in preparation of turning them to projectiles and firing them through the ceiling.

Suicide was by far the most selfish act within the scope of human behavior. There was no other action of its magnitude where the subject demonstrated how little he cared about the consequences his actions would have on those around him. There was absolutely no thought as to how the survivors would feel outside of an often vindictive need to inflict suffering, no concern at all for the well-being of brothers and sisters and parents and friends.

Generally, all it took to dissuade one of these hopeless souls was to point out what suicide would do to those who remained. Could they picture their kid brother crying himself to sleep every night, wondering what in the world he had done so wrong as to cause his older sibling to blow a hole through the top of his cranium? Could they see their mother's emotional breakdown at their funeral as she threw herself atop the casket and screamed for them to bury her as well? Could they see their father clutching at the pain in his chest as the cardiac arrest finally finished the job that the broken heart had started?

He could describe these events in vivid detail because he had lived them. And not a single day passed that he wasn't forced to endure them again. There was to be no closure, just the thumbnail that was life picking at the scab and never allowing the wound to heal.

When Darren called, Kevin had sat there with the phone pressed against his ear, unable to formulate could the words to express the maelstrom of thoughts that sped through his mind.

"...human bones," he had heard clearly. "...Kettner Lake..."

While Kyle hadn't died that night at the lake, as they suspected Melinda had, Kevin was still convinced that the reason his brother had killed himself was hidden somewhere in the mystery surrounding her disappearance. Kyle had been a model student, varsity football player, and an all-around great guy. Even now that Kevin had some understanding of the inner workings of the mind, he couldn't look back and see the emotional triggers that might have led his brother to consider suicide even in passing. No, something had happened that night with Melinda that had caused him to rush home and head directly into the garage, where he had known the shotgun would be waiting. And somewhere, wrapped in that enigma, was the truth that would allow Kevin to forgive himself, to find the closure he so desperately needed, so that maybe he'd be able to shut his eyes at night and not see the smoldering remains of Kyle's face.

There were still people who thought that Kyle had killed himself because he couldn't find a way to live with the guilt of having murdered Melinda, but Kevin knew his brother better than that. Kyle wouldn't have so much as raised a hand to her to save his own life. Throughout his high school years there had been dozens of theories about Melinda's disappearance. Some speculated she might have cheated on Kyle, and that when he found out, he had flown off the handle and butchered her into pieces so small they had been easy to hide in the marsh. Others thought she might have just swum out too far and drowned tragically, and Kyle hadn't been able to bear the grief of being unable to save her. That was the story that held the most appeal for Kevin. It made his brother and Melinda sound like some sort of modern Romeo and Juliet. There were still other rumors that she had gotten pregnant and he had made sure there was no way she was going to ruin his life by having a baby and forcing him to choose between his new family and his future. Jeff Sauers had even been more than happy to share his theory that they had been having some sort of rough, kinky sex and Kyle had strangled her during the act.

Kevin hadn't cared for that theory. Jeff had finally stopped spreading that tale after Kevin had broken his now-crooked nose.

Most everyone had thought of Kevin as some sort of social leper. None of the girls from school wanted anything to do with him, since he was filled with the same blood that just might have driven his brother to slaughter his girlfriend. None of the guys had really known what to say to him, so most of them had just turned the other direction when they saw him coming. And after he had pounded Jeff Sauers's face until it resembled a rotten tomato, they had just stopped trying altogether.

All but Darren, that was.

Darren was the only true friend that had stuck by him through the entire ordeal. He had been there to listen to Kevin cry, and he had been there to share the few fond memories from his childhood. There was no reason he should have done it. After Kyle's "accident" as his mother had called it, Kevin had retreated into himself, growing more introverted with each passing day. Yet for whatever reason—and Kevin was thankful for it—Darren had stayed right by his side, making him go hang out when he didn't want to, forcing him to go to the high school football games when he had absolutely no desire to even leave his room, and insisting that he participate in life, no matter how small the role, when all he really felt like doing was dying. It was almost as though Darren had stepped up when Kyle killed himself and assumed the role of brother and confidant. For all intents and purposes, without forcing himself to label their relationship,

Kevin did think of Darren as his brother.

And he knew that even by calling him, Darren had put his job with the police department on the line. But Darren knew he needed this. If what he theorized was indeed true, and they were in the process of unearthing Melinda Wright's body after all of these years, then maybe buried alongside her was the reason for his brother's suicide.

Yet, still, it took all of his willpower to open the door and step out into the intensifying storm. Bitterly cold raindrops patterned the side of his face, and drained in frigid rivulets through his stubble, down the slope of his neck, and into the collar of his shirt. His navy blue suit jacket was merely draped over his shoulders, as though he had haphazardly hung it there. His dirty blonde bangs clung to his forehead, and clumped into strands that betrayed the fact that his mane was beginning to thin. Small round droplets of rain clung to his glasses, dotting them like protozoans on a microscope slide, absorbing the red and blue of the spinning lights.

The ground was only now beginning to turn to mud, the formerly windswept, sandy surface softening substantially beneath the wingtips he had grabbed in his hurry to get out the door.

He walked in a daze, inhaling the sulfuric smell of the gasses burping through the slick black mud in the cattails, a scent so familiar that it was as though he had never left it behind. His arms hung at his sides. Head cocked to the right, he looked up into the cottonwoods that towered over him and noted that they had aged, but didn't seem to have grown.

A sharp poke on his neck roused him from his trance. He slapped at the source of the pain, squished a mosquito, and flicked it to the ground.

"You can't go back there," a uniformed officer said. He appeared from the mouth of the path as though from thin air. He wore a yellow rain poncho stenciled simply with "POLICE" across the front. The cowl concealed his eyes so that all Kevin could see was a mouth set above a rigid jawbone. "This is a crime scene."

"I came…" Kevin started, losing track of his thoughts as he stared into the shifting branches beyond the man. "I, um…Darren Drury…Officer Drury. He called me. We're um, old friends."

"I don't care who you are," the officer said, crossing his thick arms over his chest. He had a roll of police tape in his right hand that he had apparently been about to use to cordon off the area before Kevin had interrupted. "There's absolutely no way you're getting past me. So here's what you're going to do: you're going to turn around and walk back to that fancy sedan of yours. You're going to open the door and drag your weary ass behind the wheel, and then you're going to—"

He was cut off by the pressure of a hand on his shoulder. Whirling, he found himself face to face with another officer who leaned closer and whispered quietly into his ear. The officer nodded slowly as Darren spoke, still holding him by the shoulder.

The officer glanced at Kevin from the corners of his eyes and then looked back at Darren, who continued to speak calmly, and now gestured with his free hand.

The officer nodded and took a step back.

"Ten minutes," he said, beginning to unravel the end of the bright yellow tape. He walked to the large trunk of a cottonwood to the right of the opening to the path, reached around it, and worked the tape into a knot.

"Come on," Darren said softly. He threw his arm over Kevin's shoulder and looked past him toward the road beyond, where he would have been able to see a set of headlights for a good couple of miles. "We're going to have to be quick."

With a nod to the other officer, Darren swept Kevin onto the path and into the darkness that grabbed at him with fingers of willow leaves.

V

"We found the first one right here," Darren said, pointing to a small fluorescent pink flag affixed to a thin metal rod, which had been staked into the sloppy mud on the bank. "Some lady's dog retrieved it from out there in the lake."

Kevin stared over his burly friend's shoulder to the rain-dimpled lake, which appeared as though it were beginning to boil.

Darren's yellow poncho beaded the raindrops and channeled them into thin rivers through the plastic folds. The hood was pulled so far down over his face that all Kevin could see were his lips and his cleft chin jutting from the shadowed recesses.

"Is it hers?" Kevin asked in little more than a whisper. He cupped his right hand over his brow and watched several scuba-garbed officers splashing around in the chest-deep water. Large halogen spotlights cast a pale yellow glare on the surface of the water. The swelling droplets of rain on the Plexiglas shields covering the bulbs cast large gray shadows.

"No way of telling for sure just yet," Darren said.

Kevin was positively shaking, be it from the rain and cold or something rooted more deeply in his psyche. He felt like a wet mongrel that had crawled out of a frozen lake just in time to be beaten by his master.

"What do you think?"

Kevin looked cautiously at Darren, then back at the ground. He noticed a long cylindrical impression in the mud at the base of the little flag.

"We have two distinct skeletons. One male and one female, based on the breadth and depth of the pelvic girdles."

"There was another kid who disappeared after Melinda, wasn't there?"

"Brian Stillman."

"You think the other one's his?"

"I can't say either way. Not until we can compare dental records and DNA samples. That's our working theory, though."

Kevin sighed and raised his trembling right hand to wipe the water from his eyes.

"And they found them out there? I thought they dredged this lake back then."

Darren didn't answer. He just watched the men out in the water as they dove below the black surface and then reappeared with the stirred bed clinging to their masks in brown splotches.

Though Kevin had repressed it rather comfortably, the image of sitting there on the side of the road, watching the police rake the bottom of the lake, was now clear in his mind. As was the fact that it had been Darren sitting there quietly beside him.

What wasn't Darren telling him?

Kevin turned back to Darren, whose lips were pressed so tightly together they appeared white. He couldn't see his old friend's eyes beneath the yellow cowl, from which water streamed across the shadow of his face, nor could he feel their weight upon him.

"I just thought you might need to see this," Darren said.

Kevin watched the surface of the lake, which popped with the rain like water drizzled onto a greased griddle. He allowed his gaze to drift down the muddy bank. Directly ahead, about ten yards away, a section of cattails bowed toward the ground as though they had been recently threshed. There was a sloppy ditch just this side of them with ruggedly formed ridges that were about the width of a truck's tires.

"You could have brought me out here tomorrow," Kevin said. "Hell, you could have told me all of this over the phone."

Darren turned to face Kevin, who probed the shadows under the hood, trying to find his friend's eyes. The eyes always told the truth.

"What did you want me to see?" Kevin asked.

Silence stood between them. The raindrops began to blow sideways on the rising wind. He could feel Darren's stare on his face as easily as the cold spheres of water beating his skin.

"None of this passes your lips again. Understood?" Darren said softly. This time he tilted his chin up and allowed a distant flash of blue lightning to momentarily illuminate his spectral features.

He was a shade of pale just this side of translucent. His chestnut irises framed forks of lightning.

"What did you find?" Kevin asked.

VI

Twin bags rested side by side in the cropped buffalo grass just above the transition point between the reeds and the muddy bank. At first sight, Kevin had thought they were sleeping bags. They were about the right size. It only took him a moment, however, to discern that the zippers and the silver teeth clenched along the tracks went straight down the center, rather than along one of the sides. They were made of a slick-looking black vinyl that reminded him of the buttery leather interior of his Lexus. Water puddled in small pools on the uneven surface, as though enclosed within were irregularly spaced stones.

Darren looked up from where he crouched beside the bag on the right, and toward the wall of reeds beyond, where crunching and thrashing sounds drew his attention. Diffuse light filtered through the parallel spears from the flashlights wielded by the officers who tromped through the densely interwoven cattails in search of the missing parts. They were still waiting for the reinforcements of the canine unit. After a long moment, the light faded into the night and the crashing in the underbrush grew farther away.

"We've got to be quick," Darren said. He hurriedly reached down and jerked the zipper open with the sound of tearing denim.

A smell like freshly turned compost bloomed from within before the wind mercifully stole it.

"I don't know what you expect me to do," Kevin said, crouching like a catcher beside his old friend. "After all this time, I don't think I could even recognize Melinda."

"That's not why I called you out here."

Darren pulled the long black Mag-lite from the holster on his hip and brought it to life. The flashlight quivered in Darren's hand. He moved it slowly up the zipper and then directed it between the parted sides.

"Oh God!" Kevin said. He clapped his hand over his mouth, closed his eyes, and toppled backwards onto his rear end in the mud.

Darren merely looked at him. He'd apparently already had time to acclimate himself to the sight.

"He couldn't have—" Kevin sputtered, shaking his head violently. "There's no way. No way that Kyle... that my brother could have done...*that*."

"Kevin..."

"Jesus. God in heaven," Kevin stammered. He scuttled backwards into the reeds like a wounded crab, slipping and sloshing in the thick muck. "What happened to her eyes?"

"I knew you'd have to see this," Darren said. He pulled the zipper back into place. "You wouldn't have believed me if I'd just told you, and the last thing I would have wanted was for you to end up reading about it in the paper."

"Couldn't have…couldn't have been…Kyle…not Kyle. He…he loved her, Darren. There's no way—no way!—he could have ever…ever…"

"I'm not saying for sure that he did, Kevin. But, you know, we have to consider the possibility—"

"God," Kevin whispered, wrapping his arms tightly around his torso. Suddenly, he could feel every drop of the frigid rain tracing his flesh. He shivered. Twin lines of clear fluid drained from his nose. When he opened his mouth to speak, his teeth chattered momentarily before he was finally able to force out the words. "How could anyone have done that?"

Lightning crackled across the sky, migrating from the churning black underside of one cloud into the electron void of the adjacent.

Thunder ground the heavens with the sound of crumbling sandstone.

Darren placed his right hand on Kevin's shoulder. A faint mewl erupted from Kevin as he struggled in vain to contain his emotions. Darren looked past him and to the ground beyond, where the tire tracks leading all the way through the crumpled cattails and into the lake were still clearly visible.

CHAPTER 5

Graveyard Shift

I

The gentle buzz of the portable x-ray machine's motor echoed back to him from the deserted hallway. He clasped the wide handle of the large, rectangular unit and steered it like a shopping cart. Though the machine was self-propelled, it didn't move half as fast as he would have liked. He absolutely dreaded having to come all the way down to the basement, especially knowing what he had to do.

It was one thing in the light of day, but it was another entirely this late at night.

His footsteps pounded hollowly, stretching all the way down into the distance, where the thin corridor terminated in a dead-end at the base of the service staircase. Long strings of fluorescent tubes with just the slightest blue tint ran the length of the ceiling. They reflected back up from the always freshly waxed, white vinyl floor tiles, like the dotted white lines down the middle of a two-lane highway. The walls had once been stark white, but now had an almost dingy layer of grime on them that made them look like they were coated with a thin film of pipe smoke.

Central Storage and Supply passed on his right, the door closed and dead-bolted. The horizontal blinds were drawn tightly over the mesh–reinforced window built into the cinderblock wall. There was a little placard labeled "We Will Return At:" with a picture of a small blue clock leaning against the window from within on the sill. The little red moveable hands hung loosely so that they both pointed straight down at the six.

The next door would be on his left, and much as he would like to, he wasn't going to be able to pass it by.

Steve dreaded the ringing phone during the night shift. No good had ever come from it. Either it was the morning guy calling to say that he was going to be late or wasn't going to be coming in at all, or it was someone else in the hospital that needed his services "STAT." No one ever called for Steve personally, but that was really no different than his own phone at home. Not since Emma had left, anyway. She'd said that he'd been possessed by something that had never allowed her to truly enter his heart. Worst part of it was that she had been right, and he knew it. As each of the shrinks he had summarily dismissed had concurred, he had issues with intimacy.

That was no big shocker. He had known as much

going in. That's why he had made the appointments in the first place.

Psychiatrists were like the mirrors in poorly-lit public restrooms. They were able to draw attention to every flaw, no matter how minuscule, point out every blemish and scar, but when it came to actually doing something about it, all they could offer was the same blank stare reflected back at him.

Therapy. That was the answer. Let's talk about your problems, see if we can get to the heart of the matter.

My brother was butchered before my very eyes and they never found his body.

But he never said this. Not to anyone. Not since he had been a child.

No one had believed him back then. Not even his parents.

A flash flood had raced down from the mountains and barreled through the thin stream where Steve had been hiding. That was what they had officially concluded. Caught Brian, dragged him right down beneath, and buried him under Lord-only-knew how much dirt and debris at the bottom of that lake.

Flash flood.

It hadn't been a flood that had driven a rusted length of metal shaped like a scythe through his brother's chest. Nor had it been any kind of wave that had palmed his head with clawed fingers and broken Brian's cranium as if it had been no more substantial than a gourd. He hadn't watched his brother get carried off by a wall of water, but dragged behind some tattered-cloak-wearing demon.

Steve shook his head. All of those old images came rushing back to him when he came down into this hallway. Maybe it was the undercurrent of formaldehyde that sucked the life from the oppressive air, or the smell of smoldering bone like recently drilled teeth. Or maybe it was just that this was where the dead paused on their journey between the sunlight and stars of the world above and the earthen darkness of their eternal rest. This was where they came so that man could appraise the work of God and attempt to unravel the final mysteries of existence from the bloated intestines and the organs that remained unharvested. This was where men worked with bone saws and scalpels to decipher the code of death as if it were simply a series of components like DNA, which they could crack to prevent its recurrence in the future. This was where sloppy sutures were sewn without regard for aesthetics, as even the hemp-like twine they used to close those bodies back up couldn't have been less attractive than if they'd used lengths of bloody catgut.

This was where everyone would end up someday.

Steve inhaled a deep breath of relatively clean air for the last time and shoved the door open, turning into it to brace its weight on his right hip. He backed the machine inside and allowed the door to the dingy hallway to close, sealing him behind the thick door labeled only by the engraved plastic sign bolted to the door.

MORGUE.

II

He had just finished x-raying the facial bones of a drunken brawler with breath that smelled like turpentine and a ring of swelling around his right orbit that resembled a puffy purple donut, when the phone had rung the first time. At that precise moment, he had been in the darkroom changing out the radiographic film in the plastic cassette housing and feeding the exposed copy through the processor in the weak glow of the fifteen-watt red bulb mounted in the ceiling. Why the radiology department at North Metro Denver Hospital hadn't sprung for a digital computerized system yet was beyond him. It would have saved so much time, not to mention the repeat exams necessary due to the limited exposure latitude of traditional polyester-based film.

He knew that they'd call back if it were important enough, and besides, he needed to get that drunk out of his examination room before he wound up with puke all over the floor. Steve knew all too well who would have to clean up that mess.

The phone was still ringing when he exited the darkroom and stepped back into the dimly lit office.

"Radiology. Steve," he answered, kinking his neck to pin the phone against his shoulder. He stood beside the return tray of the processor and held out his hands to catch the x-rays that would soon roll out into the light.

"Tony around?" the voice asked.

"Nope. He's off weekend nights. You're stuck with me."

A brief pause.

"This is Alan downstairs. We're going to need you to bring down the portable unit."

Steve cursed silently and shook his head.

He pulled the film from the tray and walked it across the room to the lightboard where he clipped the top into place. From the Water's View of the skull, which was like looking straight through the face of his subject with the patient's nose tilted skyward, he could clearly see that the zygomatic arch beneath the patient's right eye had been fractured on both the zygomatic and temporal processes, the remainder displaced inferiorly into the mess of swelling.

Pasting a little yellow date sticker on the film, he slipped it into the man's file jacket and waited for the other two films to slide out of the processor.

"Can you give me a bit?" Steve asked. He glanced at the clock on the wall.

3:16 am.

"Not this time, I'm afraid," Alan said.

"Where's it going to go?" Steve asked. He smiled to himself as he pulled the next film from the processor and held it up to the viewbox long enough to label it with the date as well.

There was a brief moment where all Steve could hear was the crackle of static through the line.

"I'm going to need those x-rays STAT," Alan said, and terminated the call with a click.

Steve shrugged and hung the phone back up on the wall.

Tugging the last film from the rollers, he tacked it up against the lightboard long enough to make sure that his positioning and technique were acceptable, then stuck a date sticker to it and slid it into the folder with the others.

"You're free to go back to your suite," he said, walking back into the exam room. "From here, I'll take these films to the over to the ER docs and they'll begin planning the course of your treatment."

The man nodded. He swayed sideways as he stood and threw out his arms to steady himself. His scruffy cheeks puffed with air and his Adam's apple rose sluggishly, but with a repulsive belch, he forced his bile back down into his stomach.

Steve stood in the open doorway and waited for the scraggly man to stumble out before allowing the door to fall closed behind him. He dropped the jacket full of radiographs in the "IN" box for the emergency physician who was leaning back with his head against the wall, his mouth open wide. His snores betrayed the fact that he'd been on for close to twenty-four hours already.

Steve walked back to the department, loaded a stack of fourteen-by-seventeen and ten-by-twelve-inch cassettes into the film compartment beneath the handle and turned on the portable machine.

He hated this part of his job most of all. It was one thing taking exams on living, breathing people, but it was another entirely when he had to x-ray the dead. When he'd gone into radiography, he hadn't even given a thought to the prospect of having to perform examinations on corpses. Why in the world would they need to do such a thing? As it turned out, though, it was standard practice to perform anteroposterior and lateral projections of both the head and the chest. The skull views served as posthumous dental records and the chest images showed any sort of glaring trauma that might warrant further investigation. The x-rays were able to localize foreign bodies and metallic shrapnel, as well as acute trauma. Somewhere in the file room of just about every larger hospital was a series of x-rays of everyone who had died in that hospital. The thought was positively morbid.

At least with the living, he could force their joints to bend if he needed them to or he could get a little help through communication with the patient. Not with those bodies downstairs. By the time he got to them, their joints were usually stiff with rigor mortis, and even through his latex gloves, he could feel just how cool their skin had become. Their flesh was already blotching and working its way to transparency, and their stomachs were bloated with the gasses produced by the bacteria left alive in the intestinal tracts.

North Metro was a Level III Trauma Facility, so they didn't see the volume of ER patients that they would see at Denver General, nor would their patients be of as high acuity. Deaths in the ER were fairly rare, as the most traumatic patients they received generally were in motor vehicle accidents or suffered from non-life-threatening falls. But occasionally, someone coded on one of the surgeon's tables or suffered a fatal myocardial infarction in the ER, and downstairs they went.

This one was different, though.

From the moment Steve walked into the small reception area of the morgue, he knew…

This one was different.

III

The door was closed to the mortician's office to the right, but through the window and the horizontal blinds, he could see a police officer talking on the telephone at the desk. All Steve could see of him was that the dark hair beneath his cap was dripping wet. The water drained down the officer's neck and into the deeper blue of his collar.

Steve drove the humming cart through the small waiting area, which consisted of little more than a pair of thinly upholstered chairs set to either side of a small wooden coffee table that supported a meaty stack of aged magazines. There was a reception desk at the back of the room, adorned with a computer monitor and keyboard, and a bell with a hand-written sign that read "Ring For Service."

Usually the door leading into the back room was closed, and he'd have to stand there for half the night, it felt like, ringing the bell repeatedly until whoever was back there woke up and dragged their tail around the counter to help him. Not tonight, though. Tonight the door stood wide, and he could hear the soft echo of voices from the hollow room beyond.

Two long, stainless steel slabs dominated the middle of the room, dividing it into thirds. Mounted to the ceiling above were all sorts of surgical implements, which attached directly to the power source up above on long, retractable arms. Beside both tables were stainless steel trays, covered with twin assortments of scalpels, forceps, and hooks in large metal dividers that reminded Steve of his grandfather's old wooden toolbox. Against the back wall, matching bookcases sealed behind glass doors flanked a small, cluttered desk.

In the center of the room, enormous domed lights with reflective surfaces were positioned so that two pointed at each of the tables, focusing beams of light so bright they appeared palpable. The rest of the room was a bland silvery-gray that was uncomfortably reminiscent of the inside of a hook-filled room on a slaughterhouse floor.

A thin doorway in the rear right corner led to the refrigerated lockers.

"Thanks," Alan said. His conversation with the uniformed officer beside him had ceased the moment they heard the sound of the portable x-ray machine's motor. He wore a white lab jacket that reached all the way down to the middle of his thighs, with his hospital ID badge clipped to the tiny breast pocket. His thick black hair was streaked back with gel as always, and his face bore the eternal five o'clock shadow he surely worked day and night to cultivate.

The officer looked up at Steve with weary blue eyes so bloodshot that the rims of his lashes looked crimson. His plump cheeks matched his stocky build, his navy blue jacket framing a bulbous belly that wouldn't allow it to close. He nervously flipped the snap on his black gun holster open then closed, open then closed with an annoying clicking sound.

Steve nodded to him and approached to the tables.

On top of each of the twin steel slabs was a long, black vinyl bag.

Usually by the time he arrived, the bodies were out in the open, on top of those tables, with their lips turning a rich shade of icy blue and their pallid skin displaying the network of blood vessels beneath. The hair covering their bodies thick and wiry like unraveled Brillo. Nailbeds turning cyanotic like rising blue suns. Nipples constricting to sharp points as the blood chilled within. He generally tried not to look at their faces as the violet eyelids often showed the lumps of the irises beneath. Their mouths were often parted by their swollen tongues and the gasses building behind in the esophagus, which waited to escape in a belch.

Tonight, however, those matching bags on either table were still zipped up tight.

"Can you just do this through the bag?" the officer asked. "It took forever to get them arranged properly and I don't want to get the parts all shuffled up again."

"I'll have to move the zipper out of the way, but otherwise I should be able to slide the film right underneath the bag, no problem."

He'd never been asked to perform the examination with the body still in the bag. He could only imagine what was in there. The hacked up body of a brutally slaughtered cuckolder? The dismembered remains of a tragic MVA? He had once seen what was left of a man who took a spray of lead from a double-barreled shotgun at close range, which had punched twin holes straight through his chest and left just a worm-like strap of the mediastinum between the binocular openings. There had been another lady who'd been run down in a crosswalk. Her face had slammed so hard against the hood of the speeding car that all of her features had been smashed flat. The back of her cranium had resembled a cracked egg shell.

But both of those had been out of the bags, even though they had to be scraped back up with an implement resembling a spatula, like raw hamburger from a cold skillet.

Steve caught the officer's eyes and reached for the zipper of the bag on the table to the left, half-hoping for the officer would try to stop him. His hand trembled slightly as he pinched the zipper between his fingers and drew it slowly downward.

He wasn't sure what he had expected to see, but this certainly wasn't it.

Rather than the coppery stench of violated flesh, Steve was accosted by a cloud of the almost sulfuric scent of marsh water. It seeped out behind the zipper like an earthen mushroom cloud, rife with the biological taint of decay and recently turned earth. And what lie beneath that pungent aroma left him breathless.

The sides of the bag cast thick shadows over the remains within from the powerful overhead halogens. At first, it was like trying to look into the fathomless depths of shadows in a well on a sunny day, but the farther he drew the zipper down, the more the tines of the zippered edges parted to reveal what was contained within. Slowly, the shadows that obscured all but the most vague outlines and definition began to dissipate.

The light reflected blindingly from the skull where the eyes should have been. A rusted rectangle of metal had been strapped over the sockets and affixed in place by a series of long nails that had been hammered as far as they could go through the metal and bone, and then pounded sideways until they were flush with the cranium. The rims of the nail heads had been pounded so hard that the frontal bone had cracked and spider-webbed away from them. There wasn't a single inch of skin still attached to the featureless face, only crusted wads of mud packed into the fine crevices. The bone had lost its formerly white luster and taken on the manila tint of the pages of an ancient tome. Only the two rear molars to either side were still embedded in the upper jaw, and the entirety of the lower jaw was nowhere to be seen. Instead, a ragged length of cervical vertebrae trailed away from the base of the skull. All of the transverse and spinous processes had snapped off, and the bodies were out of alignment. Both clavicles were broken in several places, and were barely attached to a sternum that looked as though it had been hammered several times. The few remaining ribs were packed together with mud, though there was no longer any viscera to protect within.

That was as far as Steve needed to unzip the bag, so he went no further. So long as he could get clear images of the head and the thorax, then that would be the extent of his involvement. He had never produced exposures of a corpse lacking flesh and wondered if a photograph wouldn't serve the exact same purpose as a radiograph, but to ask the question would involve spending that much more time down there in the bowels of the hospital. Already he was beginning to feel as if there were invisible insects crawling all over his skin.

He produced the first of the x-ray panels and slid it beneath the bag, careful not to disturb the positioning of the skull. It needed to face the ceiling as it was, but for the life of him, he couldn't steal his gaze from that rusted strip of metal bolted to the forehead. What kind of monster would nail that into someone's face after they were dead? He paused. He could only assume that it had been done posthumously...

Gripping the handles of the extendable arm of the portable x-ray tube, Steve swung it over the skull and pressed a small black button to produce a square of light that framed the face.

"You might want to step into the other room for a few minutes," Steve said, walking back around the machine and drawing the exposure button on a long cord from its holster.

"We'll be fine," the officer said, checking his watch for the hundredth time in the last few minutes.

"Then you'll need to back away." The machine whirred when Steve pressed the button halfway, triggering the rotor to spin. "Shooting x-ray."

There was a single beep.

In that tenth of a second, the space between when he

pressed the button and the radiation exposure ended, Steve thought he saw something. He hadn't been watching carefully, merely trusting his positioning and technique and monitoring the anatomy from his peripheral vision, but he could have sworn that in that heartbeat there had been flesh covering the skull. Not just that, he also thought he had seen it buckle backward as though in a contortion of pain.

He studied it more closely, but it was the same as it had been a moment prior. No flesh, no movement. Just a skull resting between the parted zippers of a body bag.

Steve changed out the first x-ray panel, placed it back into the storage compartment of the machine, and slid a fresh cassette in its stead. Carefully, he took the skull by either side of the head, and rotated it ninety degrees to the left, so that it was facing the still-closed bag on the table opposite it. Through a crack in the parietal bone, Steve could see the sharpened end of one of the rusted nails nearly a full inch inside the head. Summoning the light field, he centered the skull within it and then backed away.

"Shooting x-ray," he said, and pressed the button.

Beeeeeep.

In that fraction of a second, Steve saw it clearly this time. Flesh appeared over the exposed bone. Jagged lacerations lined the forehead leading up to the hairline from where the nails had been pounded through the metal. A mud-crusted nest of hair appeared on the head, and the facial features filled out in the blink of an eye. A nose appeared where there had only been an inverted heart-shaped hole; lips plumped over that toothless smile and stretched into a soundless scream. The skin was covered with cracking, dried mud that looked like the bottom of an evaporated pond.

And as quickly as it had happened, the skin and features vanished, leaving nothing but the lifeless skull in the bag.

"Did you see that?" Steve gasped.

"See what?" the officer asked, again checking his watch.

"It looked like…like…"

"Are you almost through?" the officer interrupted.

Had he really seen what he thought he had, or was it all a figment of his imagination, a trick played by his mind toward the end of a long graveyard shift?

"Yeah," Steve whispered. He pulled the used film out from beneath the head and replaced it with another beneath the torso. He was going to need to raid the coffee machine for. "Yeah. Almost through."

IV

Steve waited impatiently at the return tray of the processor for the first of the films to roll out from the developer.

"Come on," he whispered, tapping his fingers on the unit.

He had seen it. He was certain of it. Each and every time he had pressed the exposure switch, in that fraction of a second, he had seen it. Every single exposure had produced the same result. The chest of that first skeletal body had fleshed out, though beneath the skin it appeared as though the ribs had been fractured to such a degree that the thorax caved inward in sections. And the second body had been distinctly female. While a rectangle of metal had been affixed over the eyes of the first skull, the second featured a bent length of rusted rebar that had been forced through the right socket and brought back out the left like a surgeon's stitching needle. The bones between were broken so severely that it looked like a lightning bolt coursing from the center of the forehead all the way down through the nose and maxillae. The nasal bones were long since gone, giving the skull the look of a split hotdog. And when he had taken the exposures, the exact same thing had happened: flesh had appeared as if by magic over the time- and weather-ravaged skeleton, and the mouth had opened into a soundless scream of unimaginable pain.

He shivered and roughly rubbed the stubble on his cheeks.

The leading edge of the first film fed slowly out through the thin slit above the return tray. Taking it between his fingers, he coaxed it out until the trailing edge cleared the rollers and rushed it over to the lightboard. With a snap, he clipped the upper border in place, and stared at the image.

Steve choked.

The flesh was still there, just as though he had taken a picture with a regular camera. Just as it had been before, the skin was raggedly torn from the puncture wounds above where the plate had been bolted over the eyes. There was a nose where there should only have been a hole and lips that framed a mouth widened by such a terrified scream that he had to stumble backwards.

The face looked horribly familiar.

As he watched, the features vanished, as though they had been composed of mist, evaporating into a nothingness that left only the skull. The metal plate was still bolted over the eyes and appeared as an opaque white strip from which the long white ends of the nails protruded like thorns. The mandible was nowhere to be seen, and only those few teeth bracketed a gaping hole in the middle of the upper row, through which he could see the fissures running along the base of the skull.

He whirled, grabbed the next film, and snapped it quickly into place beside the first. The skin was there again. From the side, he could clearly see the profile of the subject. The shadows of the tissue, like a vague white fog, were already beginning to dissociate, but he could easily discern the shape of the nose, the peeled lips stretched back from bared teeth parted in agony. He could see the outline of ears, like superimposed conch shells, and atop the crown was a tangled mess of hair.

His breath caught, and he stumbled in reverse, ramming into one of the stools and toppling it onto its side with a clatter.

"Brian," he managed to gasp. He finally lost his balance and fell squarely on his rump.

The spectral image slowly faded, leaving only the lateral image of the skull.

V

"Where did they find the bodies?" Steve asked as he burst through the door of the morgue.

Alan stood between the tables, the lights now only directed down at the table to the left, where a naked man was flat on his back on the steel slab. The zippered bags were already gone.

Alan looked up and lowered the Plexiglas shield over his face like a welder. His powder-white latex gloves were pulled up over the cuffs of the yellow smock that hung down past his knees. Black rubber boots met the floor from beneath the smock. He reached for the implement tray to his right and produced a scalpel.

"They said just to make copies of the films and they'd be back for them," Alan said. He gently inserted the tip of the scalpel right beneath the jugular notch, and drew a line straight down the center of the chest until it reached the bottom of the sternum at the ziphoid process. The edges curled back to reveal the adipose layer beneath. Blood didn't flood to the surface, but merely spread across the exposed bone.

"The bodies!" Steve shouted. "Where did they find the bodies?"

Alan raised the scalpel, slid it into the upper left side of the abdomen, and carved straight across the bottom of the ribcage where the diaphragm was hidden beneath. Feather-edged viscera bloomed from the widening incision.

"Some lake up north."

Alan looked up at Steve, but with the halogen glare reflecting from his visor, Steve couldn't tell. It appeared as though the mortician were ignoring him. Alan lifted the tip of the blade and cut another line into the right side of the abdomen. Loops of intestine slithered out like so many coiled serpents.

A foul gust of wind belched from the opened cavity.

"Which lake?"

"What's with the sudden interest?" Alan asked. He again removed the tip of the scalpel and inserted it into the center of the upper line. A spurt of blood spattered his mask. He wiped it into smears with the back of his arm, and re-inserted the knife to connect the two diagonal lines like an upside down "Y." The edges folded back as the contents blossomed from within. There was a green tint to the curls of the ileum. "Gallbladder ruptured."

"Just tell me."

Alan tossed the scalpel onto the stainless steel tray. Droplets of blood flew from the impact. He produced the bone saw and aligned it with the sternum.

"Kent Lake or something like that," Alan said. The saw screamed as it cut through the bone and created a small cloud of calcium dust.

"Kettner Lake?" Steve asked, his face pale.

"Yeah. That's right," Alan said. Fragments of bone pocked his mask. "Kettner Lake."

Steve closed his eyes. The world spun around him. His head grew light, his hands and feet heavy. It felt as though the pull of gravity had increased tenfold. Turning, he reached out both hands and tried to stabilize himself as he swayed toward the door. He couldn't breathe, couldn't recover his equilibrium. With the last of his dwindling strength, he turned the knob and staggered out into the hallway. As soon as he cleared the threshold and the door swung closed behind him, he fell to his knees on the floor.

With a moan, he let a long strand of saliva fall from his lower lip to the tiled floor, and started to cry.

CHAPTER 6

BELOW

I

April pulled the last drag from her Marlboro Light. The smoke lingered around her face, swirling playfully, before racing away on the rising wind. The cigarette fell from her fingers to the redwood deck, and for just a moment her heart leapt up in her chest. What if it singed the pristine wood? She hopped out of the patio chair and stared down at what remained of the cigarette: a mushy white filter capped with a pyramid of ash, a thin wisp of smoke snaking into the night air. So what if it left a mark? So what if it caught the whole damn deck on fire? It's not like her mom and her new daddy, Ken, would even notice. Right now, they were up in their bedroom, like they always were.

Even from outside she could hear the sloshing of the waterbed and the headboard banging against the wall. Occasionally, her mom would let out a loud moan or make a strangling sound, and April would look nervously toward the houses to either side, watching the windows for the first curious set of eyes to peek around the corner of the blinds to see what was going on.

She doubted if her mom and Ken even noticed she was there anymore.

It wasn't long after she left April's father that her mother had bought a house with Ken. There had been the six month interim during which they had lived in a two-bedroom condo with paper-thin walls, where she could remember lying awake at night, trying to block out the animalistic sounds of carnal lust coming from the adjacent room, flinching every time the bed or an elbow or head banged the wall, for fear it would simply disintegrate. That was when she had taken up smoking. Crawling out through the window to sit on the slanted roof over the carport, reveling in the car horns and other noises of traffic that masked the sounds coming from inside the house. She had tried not to dwell on the fact that her father hadn't called in weeks. Her mother had hinted at the idea that her father had been having an affair, though she never came right out and said it. Of course, they hadn't been in that townhouse more than a couple weeks before Ken had conveniently started coming by. Had they really expected a seventeen year-old not to catch on? Her mom had worked for Ken at the bank for close to a decade.

She had no idea where her dad was now. All she knew for sure was that wherever he was, he was within arm's reach of a beer and there apparently wasn't a phone in sight.

A scream pierced the night from above.

April looked to the open window of her mother's bedroom, her mind already racing ahead of her to the aluminum baseball bat she kept beneath her bed for just such an occasion. The scream faded to a girlish giggle, which metamorphosed into a guttural moan.

Her eyes raced back down to the butt on the ground. The reddish wood was scorched in a small black halo around the cherry. Clenching her fists, she drove her foot down atop the embers and dragged them from side to side until a large stain of soot marred the planks. She huffed and kicked the crumpled filter over the edge of the deck and onto the dirt yard.

Tears streamed through her thick mascara, dragging long charcoal lines down her pale cheeks. Or maybe it was the rain. She hadn't realized until that precise moment that the showers had even begun. Her jet black hair was plastered to her head. Thin rivulets of water drained through her blonde roots and rolled around the base of her ears. Silver crosses dangled from her lobes, while the tragus of each ear was pierced with a single round stud, a decision she immediately regretted the first night after being unable to jam her fingers hard enough into her ear canals to block out the sounds of her mother's passion. Her black leather jacket was beginning to fade at the seams, matching the tight gray shirt beneath, stenciled simply with the word "Naughty." A gold ring adorned her exposed midriff, the waistband of her faded jeans so low that the tops of her inguinal creases were clearly visible like the slanted ends of the letter V.

Stomping down the stairs from the porch in her oversized Doc Martens, she trudged across the muddy yard and through the lot directly behind theirs.

The foundation had already been poured, though the mounds of dirt formerly occupying its space still stood sentry to either side. From that cement pad, the skeleton of the house had risen: thin slabs of wood erected where once willows had flourished.

April walked through the open rectangle where one day there would be a sliding glass door and scuffed the mud from the deep tread of her shoes on the concrete where soon there would be carpet. She squeezed the water out of her drenched hair, flung the droplets to either side, and ascended the wooden staircase to the top floor of the tri-level, which was really little more than thin sheets of plywood nailed to the planks of wood beneath. The roughed-in walls formed a labyrinth of vertical posts that she could simply walk right through on her way to the master bedroom, where she plopped down at the edge of the room. She swung her legs out into the night, and rested her feet on the slope of the overhang above the garage. At least in here she had a roof over her head to keep the rain from bludgeoning her. At least from here she couldn't hear what Ken was doing to her mother.

"One more year," April whispered, exhuming the pack of smokes from her pocket. She brought one to her lips and shoved the pack back into the jacket.

"One more year and I am so out of here…"

She lit the cigarette. The orange glow of the cherry illuminated the inside surfaces of the wooden structure as though there were now a heart of light beating within the skeleton, and she stared out across the marsh.

Lightning forked from above, searing the night.

April slapped the side of her neck and dragged her fingers down the skin to remove the crushed mosquito.

Rain drummed with increasing ferocity on the bare plywood roof.

Not even the faintest hint of celestial light perforated the thick clouds, which seemed to swell in anticipation over the distant crests of the mountains. What little definition she could distinguish from the darkness was vague at best. Other gaunt structures stood silently from the turned earth all around, as though rising from beneath their cement headstones, waiting to be fleshed out. Thickets of cottonwoods, ringed by the fluffy whorls of the willows, swayed back and forth on the rising breeze directly ahead. The surrounding fields of cattails looked like waves rolling in on the breeze, while in the wide black gap between the trees—

Several flashes of light caught her attention. They were so far away through the thicket that they looked no more substantive than lightning bugs flitting through the reeds.

She inhaled deeply from the cigarette and watched them.

There was a sharp pinch on her bare stomach,

causing her to cough out the drag while she slapped at it in surprise.

A smear of blood remained.

She took another drag. More and more of those small lights blossomed from the trees surrounding the lake.

"What's going on down there?" she whispered.

She launched the spent butt over the roof and onto the wet driveway beneath, and clambered back to her feet, pawing at the swelling bite on her stomach.

Reflexively, her hand shot to her ear to chase away the whine of a mosquito.

In that moment, she made up her mind, and headed back toward the stairs.

II

When they had first moved into the development, it had felt as though they were right by the lake, but as more and more houses were built between, the distance seemed to grow exponentially. The paved roads faded to gravel, and the sidewalks abruptly terminated where leveled soil took over. The finished houses gave way to their skeletal brethren, which in turn were replaced by concrete poured to look as much like swimming pools as basements, and then finally by nothing more than holes in the earth.

The swampy smell of the lake, a combination of scents like mud crossed with flatus, intensified with each step. Raindrops pattered on the standing water off in the reeds, which shifted at the whim of the wind, brushing against one another like corduroy between plump thighs.

She didn't want to get too close to the lake. From her vantage, she could clearly see a handful of police cruisers parked at the end of one of the proposed cul-de-sacs. The last thing she wanted was any more trouble, so she stood there beneath the upraised plow of one of the tractors, listening to the raindrops banging musically on the metal as they pooled in the muddy basin.

Although she craved a smoke, she couldn't bring herself to occupy even one of her hands for fear she might not be able to immediately swat the mosquitoes, which felt as though they were crawling all over her. The night was alive with the sounds of humming in spite of the intensifying thunderstorm.

Beams of pale light drifted through the brush surrounding the lake in sweeping arcs, winked through the shivering leaves, and cast long shadows that bled back into the darkness.

"What are they looking for?" she whispered.

The only answer the night afforded was the chuckle and gurgle of the water rising in the gutters. It drained through the open grate built into the curb down the street, a rectangular hole that was divided in two by a single vertical length of rebar. The splashing water threatened to overwhelm the holes leading down into the sewers, which looked nearly large enough for her to shimmy inside.

Lightning flashed in the distance with an electrical crackle of static.

The surface of the lake lit up through the trees, and the falling droplets all around her appeared frozen in midair by the strobe of light.

With a thrashing sound, the field of cattails before her swayed furiously, as though some large animal was crashing through, but no sooner had the storm extinguished the light, than the sound died as well.

April slapped the back of her neck beneath the grumble of thunder.

The flashlights searching the underbrush dimmed as they grew farther away, following a circuitous route around the bank of the lake.

Lightning tore the sky again, shivering in pale blue ecstasy.

Like the fin of a shark barely breaking the surface of the ocean, a "V" raced through the center of the cattails. She was certain she heard footsteps splashing through the marsh before the thunder swallowed the sound and extinguished the electric light.

It was getting late. Or was it now early? Granted, no one at her house was going to notice she was gone anytime soon, but she was starting to feel as though the night itself was coming to life around her. The fine hairs on her arms and the back of her neck stood erect, whether prickled by the cold water that leeched through her clothes or by the static charge that lingered in the air she couldn't be sure. It almost felt as though invisible hands were trying to touch her, never getting quite close enough to graze the skin, but staying just far enough away to create a sensation of movement against it.

She spun around, half expecting to find someone staring at her, but no one was there. Only the massive holes in the earth, like so many open graves. Darkness not only resided within, but emanated without, as though crawling toward her through the teacup patterns of the raindrops on the expanding puddles.

When she turned back to the lake, several bolts of lightning laid siege to the horizon.

There was that loud splashing sound again, but by the time she divined its origin, there was nothing but a stand of shivering cattails guarding the mouth of a long cement tube, through which the runoff was funneled into a thin stream some twenty feet from the side of the road. It must have been the outlet of the overflowing drain beside her.

She smacked her cheek, hard, and winced at the sound that was soon to be forgotten beneath the thunder.

"Forget this," she said aloud. "I'm gone. These things are eating me alive."

Stepping out from beneath the tractor's plow, she nearly slipped in the slop that had merely been damp dirt minutes prior. She still couldn't figure out what they were doing down there by the lake with those flashlights, but she could only come up with one logical solution.

They were looking for a body.

The burgeoning neighborhood was filled with younger families just starting out in the world. She could easily imagine one of their little kids wandering across the street from the development into the flooded reeds, stubby little legs tripping and dropping the poor child face-first into the mire. The child would try in vain to stand, his hands sinking deeper into the silt with each exertion, until he finally inhaled that fateful mouthful of water when he tried to scream for his mother.

April shivered.

Somewhere out there in the tangled mess of cattails, an officer might stumble upon a child-sized shoe, and when he crouches to pick it up, finds it still attached to a little leg, the Osh Kosh overalls thick with mud, the body bloated with swamp water, small holes torn through the fabric where the starlings had stolen chunks of flesh.

You're letting your imagination run away with you, she thought, but that didn't stop her hackles from rising uncomfortably.

She glanced back at the reeds. The whole field jostled angrily in the storm.

Running water splashed up over the tops of her shoes.

Now she just needed to get inside and out of the storm. With thoughts of peeling the outer layers off and sinking into a nice warm bath, she urged her legs to run.

Her wet bangs slapped across her forehead and eyes, and she had to force herself to breathe through her nose to keep from inhaling the ferocious raindrops. Each footfall sounded like she was jumping into a pool.

Lightning flared. Her shadow stretched out in front

of her and jerked from side to side as the bolt snapped back and forth, in an effort to release itself from the ground like a rattler prying its fangs from flesh. The windows of her distant house glowed in reflection of the sky, like jeweled eyes through the boneyard of construction.

She felt something grab her ankle a heartbeat before she splashed face-first into the overflowing gutter. Her eyes snapped open, but she couldn't see a thing through the murky water. Mud sluiced between her clawed fingers as she fought for traction, before finally gaining just enough leverage to thrust her head back above the water with a gasp. The pressure around her ankle tightened, and what felt like nails pierced her skin. With a jerk, her legs were pulled out from beneath her and she was again underwater, and being pulled toward the drain. Kicking and flailing, April tried to break free of whatever had snared her ankle. She managed to flip over onto her back so she could at least get her mouth above the water. She dug her hands into the mud, but there was nothing to grab. Her hands simply slid through.

Both of her feet had been yanked down through the drain by the time she secured enough air to scream.

The lightning was swallowed whole by the night, and as though the lightning itself had been her assailant, the pressure about her ankle abated. Jerking her feet back out through the orifice, she scrabbled backwards, slipping and sliding in the mud, but managed to draw herself several feet from the drain before the next lance of light stabbed the ground.

There was pressure around both ankles this time,

and she was yanked quickly through the water and into the drain. By the time she was able to scream through the shock, her thighs were already sliding into the rectangular mouth. She tried to roll over, to grab hold of anything, but she was held tight.

"Help me!" she screamed, bearing down into the mud that provided absolutely no resistance. "Help—"

Her head hammered the iron lip of the drain, split in a horizontal seam across her hairline, and slammed backward into the water. The raging runoff rose up over her open mouth.

A splash echoed from beneath the sidewalk, but the crack of thunder drowned it out.

III

Darkness.

April couldn't tell if her eyes were open or closed.

Throbbing pain radiated from the swelling knot on her forehead, pulsating within the confines of her skull and reverberating down her spinal column. A copper twinge of blood dripped down the back of her throat from the pressure trapped in the sinuses behind her eyes, which felt like they were preparing to spill out of the sockets.

The cackle of running water was deafening.

She could feel it, all around her. The frigid fluid bit her mercilessly as it raced by, and it already felt as though it had absconded with her toes.

The smell of decay filled the room, aggregating into a skin of filth that coated the slippery surfaces around her.

Rolling onto her side, she tried to push herself up from the water, but her trembling hands were practically useless. The cold had turned her fingers to brittle claws, which felt as though they would snap with the addition of even the slightest pressure, but she managed to crumple them into fists and press them down into the grime until the hard concrete beneath tore the skin from her knuckles. She sputtered as churning water splashed over her face.

April managed to shove herself to all fours and vomited a flume of the wretched water. Her long hair hung down into the water as she choked on the repellant air.

She sobbed and nearly fell back into the runoff.

She was sure that her eyes were open now, for no other reason than she could feel the breeze on her bare orbs. Finally, she was able to discern the slightest definition of gray around her. Raising a shaking hand, she swiped her bangs from her face and tilted her head skyward. Twin waterfalls spewed from the gaping drain above, spilled down the layer of slime on the concrete wall, and splashed all around her. Slivers of darkness filled the gap between the ragged surface of the water and the upper rim of the drain.

Her whole body shivering convulsively, April tried to rise to her feet, but only ended up planting her face and shoulders back in the running water. Gasping for air, she fought her way to standing and staggered forward toward the wall, where she rose to the tips of her toes and reached for the outside world. Both hands passed through the engorged drainage until she could see her fingertips against the night.

Lightning pounded the ground, which trembled beneath her feet. Her fingers were highlighted against the sudden strobe of blue light, casting their shadows deeper into the tunnel to where the angled ceiling lowered to fit to the mouth of the cement tube.

A hissing sound rose above the sound of waves.

April whirled around, her vision stained by the electrical flash.

There was no movement. Nothing but the impenetrable blackness.

"Who's there?" she croaked.

The hissing sound lingered another moment, and then it was gone.

She could feel whatever was in there with her, waiting, watching. All she could hear was the running water funneling deeper into the tunnel and raining from the drain above. But she could feel it in there with her, taste it in the dead air.

"Help me!" she screamed, spinning back to the inlet. She leapt up, but her frozen legs granted her only a few inches of air. Her fingertips grazed the lip of the drain, but were unable to secure hold and dropped her back to the water. Her legs crumpled beneath her, and she fell to her knees with the water running along her bare midriff.

She whimpered and struggled to her feet again, balancing against the slimy wall momentarily before she regained her tenuous grasp on her equilibrium and jumped up toward the drain. Both hands wrapped around the middle rebar divider, which cut into her palms. Flexing her arms, she groaned and tried to plant her feet against the wall to propel herself upward, but her frozen digits slipped and betrayed her to the stream with a splash.

"Help!" she screamed at the top of her lungs. She screamed again and again, until her voice cracked, then sobbed at the pain in her throat. "Help me," she whimpered.

Her breathing became more shallow with each subsequent inhalation, each minute movement requiring more and more effort until it felt as though she could hardly hold her head up. Darkness encroached from the periphery, swarming with shadows. All she wanted to do now was lie down and close her eyes for just a few minutes. Just long enough to regain enough strength to make another leap for the outside world. Just a few minutes...

Consciousness returned the moment her forehead lolled forward into the water.

She needed to warm up in a hurry, or she was going to die down there.

The wan light above seemed so far away. She stared up at it and felt the strength leaving her body. The cold took hold with icicles driven through her skin, pinning her to the ground like stakes. Behind her, what sounded like a river gurgled through the culvert.

She turned to face downstream. All she could see of the opening was the upper arch of the black hole, through which even light didn't appear to pass. Surely it had to let out somewhere. And if her earlier speculation was correct, then it dumped out into the swamp just twenty or so feet ahead through the darkness.

She could still feel a presence down there with her. It was nothing remotely corporeal, but she could feel it nonetheless, crowding her, hunting her.

There was no other alternative.

Slowly, she placed one hand in front of the other, and crawled toward the entrance to the funnel. She had to lower her head to keep from cracking it again at the entrance, but kept it pressed firmly against the top of the tube to ensure that her mouth stayed above the rapidly flowing water. Her arched back ached as she forced herself deeper into the pipe. Choppy waves rose up over her chin, but she managed to tip it up just enough to keep the water from entering her mouth with her rasping breaths.

Time and distance lost all meaning. It felt as though she had been crawling through that claustrophobic tube for miles. Her shoulders were sore from pressing against the sides, her cramped knees and elbows in dire need of straightening, but she persevered, focusing on one hand at a time, then one leg at a time to keep the feeling of suffocation at bay.

Finally, she heard the sound of water splashing down into a larger body. A crescent of dim light appeared over the surface ahead like the last quarter of the moon.

She was nearly there.

Her adrenaline reserves kicked in and propelled her though the water. She banged her head and back repeatedly, but not even the pain was enough to slow her momentum. Faster and faster she crawled, not caring how much of the vile fluid sloshed into her mouth or how badly her palms hurt beneath the silt.

With the outlet of the tunnel no more than a few feet ahead, she sobbed and felt a swell of relief that nearly overwhelmed her. She could vaguely make out the shapes of the cottonwoods rising against the storm over the tips of the cattails.

She reached toward the opening, where the water spilled down into the waiting marsh.

Lightning struck from the sky. The sudden brightness was so blinding that she had to close her eyes against its glare. When she opened them again, a black shape eclipsed the hole leading to freedom. There was a glint of light from a hooked blade, rusted to the point that sections had crumbled away, but it was immediately swallowed by the darkness. Something splashed through the water toward her, and she screamed.

April scurried frantically backwards against the current, which tried to shove her forward toward whatever followed her. She felt the wind from the passage of slashing fingers mere inches from her face. They smelled as though they had recently been inside of something dead.

"Help!" she screamed. The crown of her head scraped the rounded cement ceiling so hard that a clump of hair tore away from her scalp. "Please!"

Progress was maddeningly slow. She wished she could turn around, but she couldn't afford to pause for even a second. Not with that thing in pursuit. Even though she couldn't see it, she could sense it coming, drawing closer and closer as she scurried in reverse.

The pressure was relieved first from her lower back, and then her shoulders. She threw herself backwards into the larger cavern where she had begun.

Immediately, she sprung to her feet and sprinted for the drain high up on the wall.

"Help!" she screamed. She leapt and grabbed hold of the lip, but her frozen arms were unable to pull her the rest of the way up. "God! Please help!"

"Where are you?" a woman's voice called from above.

April screamed in response and dropped back to the ground.

"How did you get down there?"

A hand materialized through the opening and reached toward her until it was close enough to touch.

"Take my hand!" the woman shouted.

April reached for the slender wrist and wrapped her fingers around it. Her hands were so cold that the woman's flesh felt febrile.

"Pull me up!" April screamed. "It's right behind me!"

"Just hold on tight!" the woman cried. She thrust her other hand through the drain.

April grabbed it and started to tug with both arms. She could feel whoever was out there straining against her weight. April felt herself rise several inches from the ground. She kicked at the wall to try to find some semblance of traction, but the surface was too slick.

"Please hurry!"

The woman cried out with the exertion, and raised April's feet out of the water.

April turned and looked back down the tunnel, but there was only darkness.

"You're too heavy!" the woman groaned.

"Oh God! Just pull!" April screamed.

Light flooded into the cavern from the opening of the drain, and this time when April glanced over her shoulder, she saw a dark shape sprinting through the water toward her. Tatters of fabric flagged around its form like striking serpents.

"Hurry!" April screamed back up into the mouth of the drain.

When she turned around again, the darkness was upon her. There was a flash from the rusted sickle, and then it struck the back of her left thigh like an adder.

"Pull me up!" April screamed.

Her fingers slipped from the woman's wrists as she was roughly jerked down.

"What's happening?" the woman screamed.

"God. Please. No," April begged.

The sound of ripping cloth filled the night. A sigh of air escaped through a raggedly lacerated windpipe. Hot fluids spattered the water like grease.

The thrashing water stilled.

"Talk to me!" the voice screamed from above.

There was no answer.

Downstream, a shredded leather jacket sloshed down into the waiting water. Raindrops patterned the crimson film that slowly dissolved and drifted off into the flooded reeds.

CHAPTER 7

ABOVE

I

She couldn't sleep. It was all she could do to force her eyes shut, and even that only lasted for only seconds at a time.

Lying beneath the covers, Teri stared up at the vaulted ceiling. The wooden fan slowly turned in circles on a non-existent breeze, the X-shaped shadow angling along the slanted plaster to the rectangular skylight. Drops of water swelled like parasitic organisms on the Plexiglas dome, consuming one another until the growing spheres were large enough to incur the wrath of gravity, and raced away toward the gutters. The droplets cast shadows on the bedspread, living creatures of darkness that crawled over her still form.

Lightning flashed from the grumbling storm,

simultaneously summoning a rectangle of light from above and parallel slivers through the vertical blinds covering the window. Where the warring factions of light clashed in the middle of the room, the luminescence swirled with battling motes before vanishing beneath the roar of thunder.

Bo stirred beside her, raised his head, and craned it toward the window. His green eyes flashed with amber like those of a deer. His ears folded back.

"They're still out there, aren't they, boy?" she asked, scratching behind his ears. His back was pressed against her right side, tail wagging against her ankle.

The clock beside her bed read 3:18 am.

Her mind kept drifting back to the lake.

She abruptly climbed out of bed, walked to the window, and parted a gap in the blinds. They were still out there, though the number of flashlight beams had dwindled substantially. Swirling red and blue lights highlighted a stand of trees beside the road. A pair of headlights that flashed across the front of her house before they turned back behind the bank of willows.

Another set of headlights started as pinpricks against the horizon. They grew larger as they wound around the lake and then pulled off onto the uneven shoulder. Their vacant halogen stare watched her from the distance.

Her desk sat in the corner to her right, upon which were stacks of books and a computer monitor. The clothes she had worn earlier in the night were draped over the back of the chair.

"Come on, Bo," she said, grabbing the clothes. "Let's go for a walk."

II

Teri tried to remain inconspicuous, keeping as much distance as she could from the impromptu parking lot while still being able to see what was going on. Raindrops pattered the branches above, but only managed to assault her with the occasional heavy drop. She clung to the shadows from the cottonwoods across the dirt road, with Bo sitting beside her, prepared to move at any moment, should someone see her. It looked as though the policemen were all so distracted that she could have walked into their midst without them noticing.

Three police cruisers formed a barricade between the stretch of dirt and the wilds beyond, red and blue lights alternately lighting the lower canopy of the trees. Yellow tape had been strung between the trees behind the cars. An officer in a matching slicker, who appeared to have his hands full with a small group of people, guarded the path to the lake. The headlights she had seen from her bedroom belonged to the news vans that were already making themselves at home, satellite dishes raised, cords trailing down around the poles in coils. A third had joined the first two sometime while she'd been changing. Three of the four major networks were represented, but it didn't appear as though they had gone live yet. Slicker-clad reporters barraged the lone officer with questions, though Teri could only hear the clamor of their voices, not their words. The officer obviously hadn't given them the answers they were after, as the camera crews still waited in their vans.

Bo looked up at her and let out a whine.

"Not this time," she said softly, stroking the top of his head. She knew he could smell the canine units down there in the reeds and that he wanted nothing more than to charge down there and wrestle in the mire, but he did a remarkable job of obeying and staying at her side. The police hounds crashed around in the tall weeds, out of sight, except for the rustling tips of the cattails.

She watched a moment longer, but it didn't appear as though the reporters would be able to pry the information they desired from the cop, and he certainly wasn't about to let them pass. They were at an impasse, but the fact remained that there must have been something pretty newsworthy back in the swamp for the reporters to continue battling as they were.

Flashlights crossed on the bank, then swept across the choppy surface of the lake.

It hit her suddenly. She'd have an unobstructed view of what was going on down there if she could get to the opposite bank. Granted, the officers and the forensics crew would be tiny from that distance, but at least she'd be able to see them more clearly than she could from here, with the trees and reeds between them.

"Heel," she said, taking up the slack on the leash. Bo fell into stride on her right hip as they headed down the road to the north.

III

She could see her house clear across the lake through the sheeting rain, identifiable only by the blue glow from the bug zapper. Every now and then she'd reach a point where she glimpsed the bank through the foliage. The lightning reflected from the water, briefly illuminating shadowed figures milling about on the far shore. Several had waded out into the lake.

She continued east, down what would one day become Willow Grove Lane, into the newest phase of the development. Dirty yellow earthmovers were randomly parked around a half-dozen gigantic holes at the end of the cul-de-sac. Corded joists and two-by-fours were stacked on pallets at random intervals, while the enormous, rusted footer-frames were piled on a flatbed trailer.

Wooden placards bore the house numbers in fluorescent orange spray paint, at the front of each lot, and there was a single professional billboard advertising custom homes starting in the mid-300's.

Judging by the size of the foundations, the houses they would eventually build weren't going to be much larger than hers, if at all. She knew how lucky she'd been to get in during the first phase, but until that moment hadn't realized just how much that meant to her, financially.

Teri walked to the end of road, where the rainwater overwhelmed the drain in the curb, turning the cul-de-sac into a small pond. She heard the sound of a waterfall somewhere beyond, as though the sewer were some distance below the level of the street. Off to the right, the runoff funneled out into the marshland from a cement pipe that poked out of the slanted hillside.

She was leading Bo at a trot onto the path that would bring them around to the back of the lake when she heard the first scream.

"Help!" The hollow intonation made it sound as though it originated in a cave. Teri turned and started back toward the cul-de-sac. "God! Please help!"

"Where are you?" Teri shouted, already starting to run.

There was a shrill scream in response, and Teri followed the sound to where it appeared to rise from under the street, through the long rectangular holes leading down into the sewer.

"How did you get down there?" she called, splashing into the sloppy brown water and crouching so she could try to see over the racing water into the darkness. She craned her neck until she finally saw some sort of movement and then thrust her hand into the cold water. It passed through, out of the water and to the other side, where she grasped at the air. She had to release Bo's leash and drop to her knees in order to lower her shoulder enough to fully extend her arm into the sewer. "Take my hand!"

Fingers like ice wrapped around her wrist. The initial shock was nearly enough to make her jerk her hand back out, and the sudden application of weight almost deposited her face-first into the water.

"Pull me up!" the muffled voice beneath screamed.

"It's right behind me!"

"Just hold on tight!"

Teri lowered her chest into the water, pressed her forehead against the concrete curb, and thrust her other arm through the hole. An ice-cold hand grabbed it immediately. The weight was more than she could bear. It felt like her arms were being pulled right out of their sockets. She sobbed with the strain and succeeded in lifting the girl from the ground, only to drop her back into the darkness with a splash.

"Please hurry!" railed what sounded like a frightened child. Her fingers clamped down so tightly on Teri's wrists that she lost feeling in her fingers.

Teri cried out as she put everything she had into pulling on the girl's arms. She had only lifted her a few inches from the ground before her elbows started to feel like they were going to snap and bend the wrong direction.

"You're too heavy!" she groaned, biting through her lip.

"Oh God! Just pull!"

Lightning flashed behind Teri. The resultant glow reached over her shoulders and down into the darkness. In that brief moment, she could see the girl like a snapshot. Black hair, wet and hanging in clumps. Raccoon eyes, streaks of mascara running down her cheeks. Eyes so wide with panic that they appeared ready to spill from her head. Her face was as pale as glue, her blue lips framing a pair of chipped front teeth.

"Hurry!" the girl screamed.

Their eyes locked, and Teri felt the girl's terror.

There was a wet sound like a hammer pounding mud and the sound of ripping denim.

"Pull me up!"

Teri was nearly jerked right through the hole into the sewer before the girl's fingers were yanked away from her wrists, leaving fingernail scratches all the way down the backs of her hands.

"What's happening?" Teri screamed.

"God. Please. No," the girl whimpered, her voice trembling.

Sounds like tearing paper were audible even over the thunder. There was a high-pitched scream that ended in a heavy sigh. Drops of warmth patterned the backs of her hands.

The strobe effect of the lightning ceased and allowed the darkness to pour back over her like syrup.

"Talk to me!" Teri shouted.

The only answer was the chuckle of rainwater pouring down into the sewer.

She heard a splash off the road to her right. It sounded like someone had jumped into the water, but all she could see were the tattered remains of a jacket.

Bo raced between the freshly laid foundations to the edge of the leveled dirt and barked ferociously at the wall of reeds where the jacket sank beneath the water.

A wash of light flooded over Teri, casting her shadow a good ten yards ahead onto the mud. She whirled and threw her hands up to ward off the oncoming headlights.

IV

"Help!" she screamed, and ran directly toward the car.

There was a screech of wet brakes and grinding gravel. Teri slammed both palms down on the beaded hood of the black Lexus, which reflected the lightning in oblong globules of water. The windshield wipers thumped from side to side. The driver's silhouette was limned by the red glow of the taillights through the rear windshield. His glasses mirrored the lightning as he looked at her.

She dashed around to the driver's side door, splashing through mud and water that was already over her feet and ankles.

"Please help me!" she shouted, banging on the driver's window, leaving sloppy, muddy handprints.

He cringed away from her, as though he expected the glass to explode inward.

Bo still stood at the edge of the reeds, barking feverishly at whatever was out there.

Teri grabbed the handle on the door and jerked on it, but it was locked from the inside.

"Please!" She threw up her arms in futility and turned to sprint back to where the single outlet jutted from the hillside, spewing drainage down into the marsh.

Water splashed up all around her, and her long hair, clumped in ratted locks, swatted her face.

"Wait," the man called after her. He had finally

opened the door and stepped out into the storm. "Are you all right?"

She heard his voice, but the words didn't register. All she could think of was the girl down there in the dark sewer. How had she ended up down there in the first place? Why hadn't she just climbed out the same way she had entered? What had happened to her? She had been there one second and was gone the next. The whole scene replayed in her head. Oh God, had the girl said *It's right behind me?* Her heart rate accelerated, and she started to hyperventilate. If so, was it possible that whatever it was, it was still down there?

Teri hurried across the muddy lot to where Bo stood with his ears drawn back, teeth bared, and his hair bristled down his spine. He continued to bark at the flooded field.

"Hey!" the man yelled. "What's going on?"

Teri just slid down the muddy embankment. Her feet slipped and deposited her on her rear end to skid to the bottom into a sloppy puddle. After trying several times to stand, she finally found her legs and charged toward the drainage pipe. Her right foot emerged from the mire without her shoe, her wet sock flopping like a tongue.

"Lady!" The man slid more carefully down the slant to keep from completely ruining his suit. His shoes were already covered with mud, and his trousers were soaked. "Are you hurt?"

Bo growled and raced toward the flooded stream, charging through the cattails. He arrived before Teri, every hair erect, tail standing straight out, and barked at the reeds beyond the widening pool.

Teri splashed down into the frigid water, which rose all the way up past her knees, and sloshed toward the opening of the cement drainage pipe. There was so much water firing out of the tube that she could barely see any airspace above. Grabbing the upper lip from the side, she swung her legs into the geyser, but the current was stronger than she expected. It threw her legs backward and wrenched her hands from the concrete. She didn't even have time to take a breath before her head was underwater, and she felt herself sliding through the silt. Pushing off from the thick swamp mud, she raised her head above the water and drew in a panicked inhalation that brought with it all sorts of foul marsh tastes.

"Over here," the man said. He leaned over the deeper water and reached for her.

Coughing up the vile liquid, Teri took his hand and crawled forward. He strained and groaned as he pulled her toward the shallows.

"What's happening?" the man shouted.

Teri opened her mouth to speak, but all that came out was a retching sound that brought up the last of the brown drainage.

She rolled over onto her right hip and panted as she tried to regain her breath. Her hair was clumped into muddy locks, her face covered with clots of sludge.

Bo stood to her right, rigid, head lowered, lips curled back from savage canines. He growled until it reached the point of explosive barking.

Teri followed the dog's green eyes toward the reeds, right as a bolt of lightning shredded the sky, turning night to day. There, no more than ten feet away across the flooding stream, she saw what had raised Bo's hackles. A dark shape clung to the cover of the cattails, barely discernable from the shadows. She could clearly see the bolt of electricity reflected in its eyes. The water that drained down its face shimmered just enough to betray its contours. It ducked its head, and its eyes vanished beneath a cowl sewn from the tapestry of night.

On the ground in front of it, barely visible over the rising flood plain, was what looked like a body.

It grabbed the corpse by the front waistband of the jeans and lifted it up, bending the body into an unnatural rainbow arch. The head lolled back into the water, opening a wide gash in the middle of its neck.

Teri glimpsed the word "Naughty" on the shredded remains of a T-shirt, which now barely hid a black bra and the pale white skin beneath.

The lightning died, and darkness converged from all sides. The subsequent grumble of thunder drowned out Teri's screams.

Not even the stars shined through the roiling clouds. There was only the faint stain of the headlights from the road above.

V

Bo charged ahead, thrashing through the stream before lunging out of the water on the other side, where the dark figure had been only a moment prior. Growling, he whipped his head from side to side, shook off the cold water, and raced out of sight through the cattails.

"Bo! Come!" Teri shouted. Taking a deep breath, she ran after him and splashed down into the stream, which rose nearly to the middle of her thighs. She dragged herself up onto the flooded bank beyond, sobbing uncontrollably, and crashed into the cattails, expecting to encounter the black figure carrying the corpse at any instant. What would she do if she ran into it? She knew absolutely nothing about self-defense. All she did know with any kind of certainty was that her best friend in the world was running blindly through the reeds, and she wasn't about to let anything happen to him.

By the time she caught up with Bo, he was nearly to the lake, standing rigidly in the thick cattails, staring off toward the water.

She lowered her hand and stroked his trembling back. He flinched and looked up at her before returning his attention to the choppy lake.

A cloud of mosquitoes hovered over the bank, which was absolutely covered with them, like black sand. It was unnatural for the insects to be out in the middle of a storm. Usually they bedded down until the rain stopped before venturing out to feast upon anything warm-blooded.

Teri stepped out onto the shore and placed her right foot on a writhing mat of mosquitoes. They squished beneath her heel. All of the other bloated insects were startled from the ground into a humming swarm around her. There was a black pattern on the brown sand like a swatch of oil on a garage floor. She knelt cautiously and placed her palm on it while the insects buzzed angrily around her head.

It was still warm.

A bolt of lightning lit the night.

The cattails rustled twenty yards up the bank before slowly coming to rest.

And then there was no movement at all.

CHAPTER 8
FULL CIRCLE

I

Kevin stood in the marsh, his loafers no match for the standing water and muck. He unconsciously wiped the mud from his hand onto his slacks. He had absolutely no idea what was happening.

There had only been one road around the lake the last time he'd been here a decade and a half ago, so he had quickly found himself lost, following the winding streets with the hope that they would lead him back to the main road. When the asphalt had faded to gravel, he had known he was definitely going the wrong way, and had just veered into the cul-de-sac to turn around when his headlights had latched onto a shadow. At first he had thought it was a large dog drinking from the engorged puddle at the end of the lane, but when it had leapt up onto two legs and raced toward him, he had slammed the brakes and prayed he wouldn't hit the wild-haired shadow.

All he remembered were wide, panicked eyes, set into a face made of mud, as she pounded on the hood and then on his window before she sprinted away from his car and into the marsh.

Now here he was, again standing on the shore of Kettner Lake, a third of the way around the bank, from where he could still see the hint of police flashlights through the distant cattails, as they searched for more bones to add to the collection they'd already removed from the site. He couldn't believe they actually suspected that Kyle could have been responsible, even for a minute. The other kid, Brian, had died several days after his brother had taken his own life. They couldn't possibly believe that Kyle had killed the other kid posthumously. He needed to take a step back and approach the whole situation from a logical perspective. First, they didn't yet know with any kind of certainty that the remains they discovered belonged to Melinda and Brian. That was just their working theory until the bodies were positively identified. He doubted it was coincidental that two people disappeared in the lake years ago and now they had discovered two distinct, disarticulated skeletons. Why had Darren summoned him then? He hated suspecting his best friend of having ulterior motives, but he was certain that there was more to it than just offering him some form of closure. That was why Darren had kept his eyes hidden. He knew Kevin could read him like a book, whether using his psychological prowess or just many years of personal experience. Had Darren called him all the way out here to gauge his reaction? No…Darren knew him every bit as well. If his reaction had been all Darren was looking for, he could have gleaned it from his voice over the phone. There was another reason…but what?

He was thoroughly soaked, his body prickled with goosebumps that ached in the cool breeze. And here he was, right in the middle of a nightmare stolen from his childhood.

Lightning tore the sky, which flashed several times as bolt after bolt crackled from one grumbling cloud to the next. A clap of thunder shook the ground. He could see his car up there on the road, still idling right where he had left it. All he had to do was ascend the muddy slope, climb in, and drive away. Instead, he looked at the wall of reeds, which shivered slowly back into place behind the woman's passage. With one last glance back to his Lexus, he turned, slogged through the runoff, and thrust both arms out in front of him to part the cattails.

II

Was she crazy? That had certainly been his initial assessment, but he figured that under the right circumstances, anyone could be driven from their right mind. He'd seen it happen on more than one occasion. Perfectly sane and "normal" people cracked under the weight of an unbearable load of stress and turned up wandering the streets days later, rummaging through the garbage. One could never predict when someone was going to snap, and certainly not in which manner, but this woman had borne an odd sentience in her eyes rather than the hollow look of vacancy.

Maybe he'd decided on some level that she was in control of her faculties and might need his help, or perhaps she was just one more part of the mystery surrounding the lake, the part that might somehow answer the questions that had burdened him since childhood.

Wet reeds slapped his face, and cottony seeds exploded from the ripe cattails as Kevin ran blindly, trying to follow the woman's barely discernable path. Fierce barking erupted directly ahead, guiding him onward until he burst through the foliage and onto the muddy shore.

He didn't even have time to formulate his thoughts before the cloud of mosquitoes swarmed around his head.

"Jesus," he gasped, swatting madly with both hands.

The woman was staring across the lake at the point where her dog seemed to be directing its barking, but he couldn't see anything over there but the darkness residing in the swaying reeds.

"I saw her," the woman whispered.

He was unsure if she were talking to him or herself, so he held his tongue. She was silhouetted against the horizon as still as a statue. Finally, she turned to face him.

"She's gone," she said, her brows furrowed, face caked with mud.

"Who?" Kevin asked. "Will you just tell me what's going on?"

The woman looked through him, her eyes growing distant.

"She was down in the sewer. I heard her screaming... screaming for help. I...I could see her down there. Through the water. She was so scared." She started to sob, raised the backs of her hands to her eyes, and smeared the tears into clear spots on her temples. Her words deteriorated to the point that he could barely understand her. "I tried to reach her. I had her hands...but I wasn't strong enough to pull her up. I couldn't pull her up."

"Then she's probably still down there."

"No," the woman whimpered. "It had her. She said it was coming for her, and it got her."

"What got her?"

"It was holding her by the front of her pants. She... she wasn't moving and her neck, oh God, her neck looked like it was cut nearly all the way through."

"What do you mean, 'it'? Who's this girl? You aren't making any sense. Slow down. Take a couple deep breaths. Then try aga—"

"I found the bone. Bo brought it out of the lake and I was...I was just going to... They'd been down there so long. I was just going to see what they were doing—"

"Who? The police?" he interrupted.

"I thought if I went around to the far side that I'd… that I'd be able to see what they were doing across the lake, but then I heard that poor girl screaming…"

Her words trailed off. She buried her face in her hands, shoulders heaving convulsively.

Kevin reached out to her, but she took a quick step away. She sniffed and swiped the mucus from her upper lip.

"Everything is going to be all right," he said. "We'll just go back and you'll see that if there really was a girl—"

"Really was a girl? You think I'm making this up?" Her eyes narrowed. "Look at this!" She stormed over to the discolored patch of sand. "What do you think this is, huh? Where else would this blood have come from?"

"I'm sure you thought you saw a girl down there, in the sewer you say? But I think—"

"What are you? Some kind of shrink?"

"Actually…yes."

"Oh, great," the woman said. She threw her hands up to her sides and let them fall to her thighs with a clap. "While you're wasting your time trying to psychoanalyze me, there's something out here with us that just killed a young girl."

He stared into her furious eyes. She believed every word she was saying.

"We should call the police then," he said evenly, watching for her reaction.

"Thank you. It's about time."

With one final glance over her shoulder, she brushed past him and crashed into the reeds. The chocolate lab growled across the lake at something apparently only he could see, then turned quickly, tucked his tail between his legs, and scampered after his master.

"Okay," Kevin sighed.

With a shrug, he looked across the lake, toward the stand of cattails that had held the dog's attention, then shook his head and followed the woman through the underbrush toward the road.

III

"I know what I saw."

"I'm not disputing that with you," Kevin said. "I know you're convinced that you saw this girl. I'm just asking you to consider the possibility that what you saw might not have been a girl."

"And I suppose I made up the sound of her screaming."

"The mind often rationalizes things in generalizations. In this instance, it's possible that since your brain didn't immediately recognize the sound, it interpreted it as screaming. Your mind has the ability to change your perception of an external stimulus so that it makes sense to you. For example—"

"Wait a minute," the woman snapped. She took a moment to calm herself as much as she possibly could under the circumstances. The Lexus' heater blasted across her wet clothes as she sat in the passenger seat. Kevin had called Darren as soon as he returned to the car and had been kind enough to invite the woman inside to warm up. He'd draped the seats with the emergency blankets from the trunk over the pristine seats first, of course. She obviously felt uncomfortable in the surroundings, as though this were some form of mobile Freudian couch he used in his practice. "Quit talking to me like I'm a child. I have a doctorate in engineering, for God's sake, which, I believe, is more than you have to have to be a practicing psychologist."

"I have a master's degree in—"

"It doesn't matter," she said, leaning across the seat toward him and causing him to flinch. She sighed and sat back in the seat. "Whether you believe me or not, there was a girl down there. I don't know her. I didn't even get a good enough look at her to tell if I'd ever seen her before. All I know is that she was down there and she was terrified. She only wanted to get out. And I couldn't help her."

"Okay." He leaned away from her, but allowed his hand to drop from the door handle. "Let's suppose for a moment that everything you've said is the absolute truth—"

"Which it is."

"Humor me, please."

He waited a moment for her to reply. She finally gave a curt nod.

"Let's start from the beginning. Earlier tonight you found what you believe to be a human ulna down by the lake, and you immediately called the police. After they'd been down at the lake for several hours, so you became curious and wanted to see what they were doing. For argument's sake, let's say they found the skeletal remains of two distinct individuals—"

"Did they?" she gasped.

Kevin watched in the rear view mirror as one of the cruisers across the lake peeled out onto the main road, blue and red lights staining the willows.

"Please," he said, holding up a hand. "You said you saw the man who took this girl."

"I can't be sure that it was a man. It looked more like a living shadow. It seemed to be radiating darkness…if that makes any sense."

"Were there any recognizable features?"

"That's just it. No. He was simply black, though he did look like he was wearing some sort of tattered cloak."

The police car turned down the street leading to the cul-de-sac, and the driver hit the brights so he could push the speedometer.

"Please," he whispered, pleading with his eyes. "Tell me again what you saw."

"You don't believe me anyway. What's the point?"

"Sixteen years ago, my brother's girlfriend disappeared at this very lake the same night he killed himself. It's possible that one of the sets of bones might belong to her. If you really saw something, I need to know."

She looked down to her lap, wringing her hands. When she finally spoke, she looked out the passenger window at the side mirror. The police car's cherries reflected on her face as they increasingly brightened the night.

"There wasn't anything to see."

"Please try."

"It was as though the night itself had taken the general shape of a man. The tatters of his cloak flared on the wind like tendrils. He had no face, just the darkness, though I could tell that he was looking directly at me. He held the girl with one hand, and in the other what looked like a long piece of rusted metal."

"Like a knife?"

"No…it was longer. And arched."

"Like a sickle."

"Yes."

"So you're telling me you saw a man in a black cloak carrying a sickle."

Kevin couldn't believe he'd bought her story for a second. Either she was really good at lying or he just wanted so badly to believe her, to believe that there could be some sort of link between what she thought she saw and what might have happened on that night so many years ago.

He shook his head to chide himself, removed his glasses, and rubbed the bridge of his nose.

"You're telling me that you saw the Grim Reaper," he finally said.

"I know how it must sound—"

He cut her off with the sound of the opening door and stepped out into the rising wind. The rain still blew sideways, though the drops were now much smaller. Kevin quickly regretted the decision. He wrapped his arms around his chest to combat the goosebumps as the police cruiser pulled in right next to him, highlighting the globules of rain on his glasses with red and blue.

IV

Teri watched from the passenger seat as the officer climbed out of the driver's side door and walked around the hood to meet up with the other man. She could only see the cop's mouth and chin beneath the hood of the yellow slicker he had pulled all the way over his head and down to his eyes. The men stood close enough to each other that she was sure they were whispering. Every so often the man would turn and look at her, triggering the officer to do the same. Right now he was probably telling the policeman how the girl in his car was completely insane. She knew what she saw though, and could still see it clearly in her mind.

Her emotions were out of her control. She alternated between fear and anger, and was just about to clamber out the door and let them both have a piece of her mind when the cop turned away from the other man with a nod. He walked around the front of the car and stood right next to her door. All she could see was a wall of yellow with the word POLICE stenciled across it. A hand rose into view and rapped softly on the glass.

Teri opened the door and climbed out, suddenly well aware of just how cold the wind had become. The brunt of the storm had passed, leaving just the flickering glow of lightning on the horizon and the diminishing black rain-clouds overhead.

"Officer Drury," he said, as if that were introduction

enough, and produced a small yellow pad and pencil from somewhere beneath the poncho. "I understand you were the one who found the bone by the lake. Is that correct?"

"Yes."

"What are you doing out here now?"

"I just wanted to see what was going on down at the lake."

"This is now a police matter, ma'am. The safest and most helpful thing you can do as a private citizen is stay in your home and let the professionals do their job."

"I didn't come down here to—"

"Now, I understand you believe you might have witnessed a homicide down in the sewer."

"Yes."

"Can you tell me what you were doing down in there?"

"I wasn't down in the sewer."

"Then how did you see this murder?"

"Through the storm drain over there," she said, pointing toward where the drain was finally catching up with the once overwhelming water. The pond had dwindled to a small puddle, and only a trickle flowed in the gutters.

"You saw a murder through that drain."

"That's what I said."

"There was a girl?"

"Yes, but I didn't get a very good look at her. Are you going to go down there and look now?" She let out a frustrated sigh.

"Of course, ma'am," he said.

He was patronizing her, which she couldn't understand, considering what they'd found down by the lake. Surely the prospect of a murder at the same place where they'd found skeletal remains would arouse more suspicion, unless for some reason they thought there might be no foul play involved.

Officer Drury had just turned his back to her and pulled out his Mag-Lite when she stopped him.

"What do you think happened to the people to whom those bones belonged?"

"More than likely drowned," he said.

She could tell he was lying.

With a nod, he turned back toward the end of the cul-de-sac and walked toward the drain. He clicked on the light and tried to direct the beam down through the twin rectangular holes, but only succeeding in lighting the water. Crouching, he tilted his head to the left and shined the beam down into the sewer.

V

Darren knew the woman had already had a long night. Everyone reacted differently under duress. Maybe this was how she handled the strain. Sure, it was possible that she had seen a girl down there. He couldn't completely dismiss the notion, but it seemed delusional. She finds a bone down there in the swamp, and next thing you know she's seeing murders everywhere. What she didn't know was that, even though they had found the skeletal remains here, they'd been transported from somewhere else. Someone had done so recently, as evidenced by the tire tracks on the bank, which ran in a direct line to where they had exhumed the majority of the remains. He had a hunch that any killer who'd been patient enough to hide the bones somewhere else for sixteen years without leaving any clues wasn't the kind of guy who was just going to back his truck up to the lake and dump them. They weren't dealing with a serial killer. Whoever had dumped the remains in the lake had done so not caring whether or not they were ever found. But surely they had hoped it wouldn't be this soon. It would have to have been someone who found the bones accidentally and feared calling the police for one reason or another. If he could just come up with that reason, he could track down whoever had discarded the remains and potentially find out what might have happened to the victims.

It was a long shot, as all he had to go on were tire tracks, but if they hadn't been cautious enough to cover their tracks, then surely the other officers would find some other clue they had left behind.

That was what he should have been doing now instead of trekking all the way across the lake to investigate a murder that had supposedly happened within a couple hundred yards of half of the entire police force. Heck, as he walked toward the sewer drain, he could see the other cruisers between the cottonwoods and the occasional flash of light from one of the canine cops. No one would have been stupid enough to even attempt to kill anyone this close to so many policemen. He'd just flash his light down there into the darkness, let the woman know that everything was okay and that it was under control, and then take her back home, so he could get down to the real investigative work.

He flicked on the long black flashlight and directed the wide beam down toward the gurgling holes in the curb. Brown water raced past and echoed hollowly as it splashed down somewhere below. He swept the light from side to side, showcasing a mess of garbage and weeds tangled around the rebar post separating the holes. There was a cement wall covered with green sludge at the farthest reaches of the beam, but that was all he could see from his current vantage.

Dropping into a catcher's stance, Darren leaned as close to the ground as he could without having to kneel in the muddy water, and shined the beam through the hole to the left. He traced the slanted ceiling back to where it terminated in a black hole, through which the water funneled into the swamp. There were all sorts of tumbleweed pieces mixed in with the long line of slime and trash in the thin stream that led away from the widened pool where the rainwater splashed down from above.

He squinted and leaned closer.

What was that? It looked like there were rivulets of oil draining down the walls. The fluid shimmered when the flashlight's beam touched it.

"Jesus," Darren gasped, throwing himself backward. He landed in the puddle on his rear end with a splash.

He looked back over his shoulder at the woman, who clapped her hands over her mouth and started to sob.

VI

They'd already found a leather jacket several yards downstream, wedged against a stand of reeds. Slashed to ribbons. The canine units followed what little scent they could obtain from the jacket through the cattails, while the beams from their handlers' flashlights knifed through the marsh.

Darren wished he'd thought to bring his hip waders as he crawled deeper into the cement tube. The running water was only about eight inches deep, but it was so cold that it felt like it gashed him with razor blades as it raced past. He held his flashlight in his right hand, doing his best to keep it above the water so he could see as far ahead as possible. He half expected to crawl onto a bloated corpse wedged in the culvert.

Flashlight beams highlighted the end of the tunnel ahead, crossing back and forth as they scoured the sewer from above. He doubted they could see much more than he could when he had been up there.

By the time he reached the inlet and the small room beyond, he was sure that every part of him that had been submerged would soon turn black with frostbite.

Except for the twin rectangles of wan light that traced the slanted ceiling, and the flashlight beams directed down at him, the darkness was complete.

There was a humming sound all around him that he assumed to be the sound of the water funneling through the grate, mutated by the strange acoustics of the enclosure.

He stood, grateful to be off his hands and knees and out of the water, and looked up through the drain at the street. Muted moonlight illuminated the upper half of his face as he jerked the hood from his head. This tomb was making him claustrophobic enough without that cowl covering his face and lending the sensation of being smothered.

"Toss down the camera," he shouted to the men above.

"I take it you didn't find a body," Officer Nelson called down.

"No such luck."

"That's a good thing."

Darren turned a slow circle and inspected the walls with his flashlight beam. Spatters of blood marred nearly every available surface as though sprayed by a hose.

"There's blood everywhere," he called up. "There has to be a body."

"The runoff must have carried it into the swamp."

"Surely the dogs would have found it by now."

"You think whoever did this took the body, then?"

Darren froze and bit his lower lip. It would be entirely too coincidental, but if they weren't able to find her body out there in the swamp, then they would be forced to consider it. Was it possible that whoever had killed this girl and absconded with her body was the same person who had murdered Melinda and Brian all those years ago? The pattern certainly fit. The only way he was going to be able to connect them was to locate the person who'd found and dumped their bones.

"Heads up," Officer Maxwell said, carefully extending his arm to hold the camera above the water. He waited until Nelson's beam highlighted Darren's face before dropping it.

Darren went back to the middle of the room and trained his circular beam on the wall directly ahead, which was coated with green slime beneath a layer of running water. He focused the camera on the fingernail marks clawed through the sludge and the scraped areas lower, which looked almost like footprints. He pressed the button, and the flash lit the room, startling a swarm of mosquitoes to flight.

Swatting through the cloud, he began the arduous process of photographing all of the blood on the walls, despite the insects settling onto the fluids to gorge themselves on the girl's pain.

CHAPTER 9
THE GATHERING

I

Steve threw his black Intrepid into park as an afterthought in his hurry to leap out the door. The dirt road was cordoned off with yellow police tape. A patrol car was parked behind the tape as a more effective physical barrier. News vans had turned road into a parking lot. Several reporters badgered the lone officer, who held them off from beyond the tape with his outstretched arms and answers that were cryptic enough not to betray what little he knew.

There were three more police cars parked down at the end of the cul-de-sac, fifty yards away, with their cherries swirling. Dark silhouettes flirted in and out of the light, occasionally illuminated by the flash of a camera. An ambulance was parked behind them, its bumper nearly kissing that of the sedan in front of it. No siren wailed, but the red lights still whirled on its roof. The back doors stood wide, a square of artificial light against the night that framed the outlines of two people sitting with their legs hanging over the fender.

Steve took all of this in at a sprint. He'd begun hyperventilating after turning off the highway, his thoughts a blur. The world around him felt surreal, as though he were in some sort of fever-induced fugue. All he knew was that seeing his brother's face on the x-rays had brought all of the old memories rushing back to overwhelm him.

He grabbed the police tape near the fire hydrant, slowed, and lifted it just enough to duck beneath, before resuming his mad dash toward the end of the street.

"Hey!" the cop called after him over the ruckus of the reporters.

Steve didn't even hear him. His sole focus was on reaching the police officers down there and making them tell him the truth.

One of the cops ahead turned at the sound of the commotion and ran right at Steve. He lowered his shoulder, cleaved Steve off the ground, and slammed him onto his back.

"Get off of me!" Steve shouted, trying desperately to squirm out from beneath the officer's weight.

"You can't be back here!" the officer shouted. "This is a crime scene!"

Steve brought his knees up with all of his might, and staggered the cop, who rolled onto his side and curled into fetal position.

Before Steve could scramble to his feet, his scrub pants now torn at the knees, revealing bloody, gravel-pocked smears, another officer was right in front of him.

"Freeze!" the man commanded, thrusting the barrel of a nine-millimeter right into Steve's face.

The sobering effect of the gun allowed the world to crash down upon him, and he began to cry. Shoulders shuddering, he dropped his chin to his chest and felt the teardrops run to the tip of his nose.

"Wait a minute," another man said. He walked up behind the officer and placed a hand on his shoulder. This man was wrapped in a blanket from the ambulance. "I think I know him."

Steve raised his head and looked at the man. His own image reflected back at him from the man's glasses.

"Stillman, right?"

Steve's features crinkled as he tried to draw the man's face from the shadows. He looked familiar, but Steve didn't immediately recognize him.

"Yeah…how did you know?" Steve whispered.

"Kevin Weatherly," he said.

His eyes locked on Steve's.

As soon as Steve heard the name, he knew. Kevin had been a grade behind him in school, and they'd never really hung out, but they had shared an unspoken bond.

"Kyle's brother," Steve said.

"This is a crime scene!" one of the officers said. "You get your tail out of here right now or so help me I'll—"

"Maxwell," another officer interrupted. The two conferred quietly while Steve still knelt in the mud, watching them intently. The world drew in and out of focus as his emotions had their way with him. With one breath he wanted to scream, and with the next, to bolt past them to see where they had found Brian's remains. The officer training the gun on him slowly lowered it until it pointed at the ground, though he still gripped it tightly in both hands, his arms tensed in preparation of raising it again, should Steve even flinch. The other approached Steve, and studied him through eyes that appeared to miss nothing. "I'm Officer Drury. Darren Drury."

"Darren Drury," Steve repeated. He slowly rose to his feet while watching Maxwell from the corner of his eye. "The same Darren Drury who used to live down off Old Wadsworth?"

Darren nodded, pleasantries through. He looked at Kevin before turning back to Steve.

"What are you doing here?" Darren asked, voice level, eyes narrowed.

"You found my brother, didn't you?"

Darren spun to look at the other policemen milling around behind him. Maxwell offered him a shrug and holstered his pistol.

"Where did you hear that?" Darren asked. He lowered his voice and took a couple steps forward until he and Steve were uncomfortably close.

"So it's true?"

"Shh! Where did you hear that?"

"I'm an x-ray tech. I work at the hospital where you guys brought the bones. I x-rayed the skeletons for standard posthumous records. When I…when I first exposed them, I thought…I was sure that I saw flesh on the bones in that fraction of a second of radiation. But it wasn't until I developed them back in the department that I knew for sure. I saw my brother's face on those films. Sometimes soft tissue shows up on the radiographs. My brother's face was right there until it faded away to leave just the skull. I swear to you. I saw Brian's face. There was no mistaking it. And he looked…he looked like he was in so much pain…"

"You could see the flesh on their bones when you exposed them to x-rays?" a woman asked. She was bundled tightly in blankets, her hair matted with rainwater and mud.

"Yeah."

"And then on the film."

He nodded. "Who are you?"

"Teri Gardener," she said. She looked as though she'd tried to proffer her hand from beneath the blanket but couldn't figure out how to get it out. "You could for sure only see the skin when the bones were directly exposed to radiation?"

"Yes!" Steve snapped. Who was this lady anyway? He turned to Officer Drury. "Show me where you found him. Show me where you found my brother. Please."

II

The sun rose from the horizon like a blooming tulip, chasing away the last of the lingering stars with orange and gold watercolor smears, which reflected from the tranquil lake like a shimmering mirror. What little remained of the storm was barely visible over the tops of the cottonwoods to the southeast, though its memory endured in the fresh scent of rain and the foliage blossoming with gratitude. In that moment, Steve was an eleven year-old kid standing on the bank with his brother, preparing for the greatest afternoon of fishing in history, but when he looked down, all that was left of Brian were small pink flags in the shallows, marking the spots where they found his bones, and the matching bobbers that floated atop the water, where the rest of him had been exhumed from the mud and silt.

"This was the last place I saw him," Steve said. His eyes glazed over as he stared across the lake. Through the years he'd come up with dozens of things he could have done differently that might have kept his brother alive. He relived them as he studied the spot twenty yards out, where Brian had presumably been carried by the floodwaters, to be entombed in the muck. He tried to remember if he had seen the raft and the divers in that precise spot so many years ago, but even if he had, it didn't matter now. "Was the other body Melinda's?"

"That's our working assumption until the lab is able

to provide positive identification," Darren said.

Steve just nodded and stared blankly ahead while the ducks and geese broke the morning's serenity.

The sounds of construction replaced nature's tune with the tinny sound of pounding hammers and the distant grumble of earthmovers. Small bursts of dark exhaust drifted into the sky on the other side of the trees to the north.

"I wish I had something more concrete—" Darren started. He looked back to the left, toward the racket of progress. His brow furrowed. Then in a whisper, "Concrete."

"What?" Kevin asked.

"You guys will have to excuse me," Darren said, looking down to the ground. He stared at what appeared to be wide tire tracks through the reeds. "I'll check back in with you later if I hear anything new."

And with that he was gone. The crunching of cattails trailed him toward his cruiser.

"What just happened?" Teri asked.

"I don't know," Kevin whispered. He watched the swaying reeds slow and finally come to a halt where his old friend had just passed through.

He picked up a flat stone from the bank and skipped it off to the left, away from the markers. After three skips, it sank with a *sploosh*.

Kevin had always known that eventually this day would come. He had no idea what he'd expected to find, but this left him feeling even more hollow than he had before. They knew nothing more now than they had before they found Melinda's remains. The evidence indicated that she had been tortured, but he knew his brother wasn't capable of doing something like that. Had Kyle witnessed it, then? Had he been unable to save her? Now, a single answer had generated even more questions that he would be forced to think about every day for the rest of his life.

"Maybe I was wrong," Steve whispered, turning from the lake. His cheeks glistened with tears. He offered them a wan smile and started walking toward the path.

"Wrong about what?" Kevin asked.

"Everything," Steve said, shaking his head.

"Wait," Kevin said more sharply then he had intended. He grabbed Steve by the arm. "You said you were here with your brother the night he disappeared."

"Died. The night he died. I'd been holding out hope for all these years that somehow… So long as they couldn't find his body, he couldn't really be dead, right? Well, they found him."

"Tell me what happened that night."

"It doesn't matter now. They found my brother's bones scattered in the middle of the lake. I've done everything in my power to keep from mourning him for the last sixteen years. I've got a lot of catching up to do."

He looked down at the hand holding his arm, then back up at Kevin.

The canine units no longer thundered through the underbrush, and the detectives had taken the pictures they needed and removed all of the evidence. There was only a single cruiser left down at the end of the cul-de-sac, there to discourage people from trampling through the crime scene until they formally closed the case.

"Please," Kevin said, looking Steve right in the eyes. He still held the man's arm, though he allowed his grip to loosen. "Please tell me what you remember. All I want is to know why my brother killed himself, so that maybe I can sleep at night without waking to the report of a shotgun in my dreams, so that maybe I can close my eyes without seeing Kyle's blood dripping from the ceiling, so that maybe…maybe I can forgive myself for not being able to stop it."

His eyes shimmered with tears.

Steve held his gaze for a long moment.

Teri walked a couple yards up the bank, to where Bo was sitting patiently with a stick in his mouth, waiting for her to acknowledge him. She was exhausted and ready to go home. The cops would call her if they needed anything else, as she'd already filled out her statement. She'd just throw the stick out into the lake a few times and then welcome the respite of sleep in the coziness of her own bed.

"We came down here after they called off the search for Melinda," Steve said. Kevin let go of his arm. "I think Brian thought we'd crack the mystery ourselves, you know, like there'd be some clue the police missed. The fishing rods were a ruse, I'm sure, but since we didn't stumble upon anything, we just fished. It was the best afternoon fishing that we'd ever experienced in our lives. We lost track of the time, and before we knew it, the sun was setting, and we needed to hurry back before our parents got home. And the storm was rolling in so fast…"

Steve raised his eyes to the sky. He bit his lower lip and waited for the quiver to leave his voice before he resumed.

There was a soft splash, then a much louder one as the retriever plunged into the water.

"We found this place, this little patch of dry ground beneath a tangle of trees. There were bones everywhere. Squirrels nailed by their tails to the trees. Their blood dripped into bull skulls that were staked into the ground by the horns. And there was this… man. This man in a tattered black cloak…"

Teri froze, and her blood ran cold. Slowly, she looked over her right shoulder at the two men.

"We tried to run from him. Each time the lightning struck, we could see that he was gaining on us, but it was so dark that we couldn't even see him without it. Brian made me hide in a drainage pipe while he tried to get help, but the man found us. We were going to make a run for the dairy, but…the lightning…and Brian's blood splashed into my eyes. The man drove a piece of rusted metal all the way through Brian's chest from behind, then grabbed him and dragged him off before I could even try to help. They just disappeared into the cattails…"

He let out a meek sob before composing himself again.

"A man in a black cloak," Kevin said evenly.

Steve nodded.

Kevin turned and looked at Teri. All of the color had drained from her face. The dog prodded her thigh with the stick, but she seemed oblivious. She just stared at Steve with her mouth open.

"Yeah," Steve said, reliving the memory in his mind. "But that's all I remember about him. Everything was just black. I never saw his face or anything. After so many years, I've begun to wonder if I ever really saw him at all, or if I'm just going crazy."

"Did the tatters of his cloak waver like snakes?" Teri asked.

"I don't remember."

"Did it look like he was the source of the darkness, rather than wearing it?"

"This was sixteen years ago. I only remember a man in a black—"

"Was he carrying a long, rusted scythe?"

The memory hit Steve like a gunshot. He saw a flash of silver tear through his brother's chest, the blood hitting his bare eyeballs before he even had time to blink.

"You aren't crazy," Teri said. "I've seen him too."

CHAPTER 10

FOUNDATIONS

I

Darren sat in the squad car at the end of the dirt road, watching the activity through a stand of willows. He was no longer on the clock. This was his own time. The only thing he was missing out on was sleep, and right now there was too much adrenaline and caffeine racing through his system to even consider the prospect. So long as he caught a quick snooze in the afternoon, he'd be fine to go back into the station at seven that night.

The more he thought about the idea, the more it made sense. If they'd unearthed the skeletal remains in the process of excavating a foundation, then involving the police would have turned the area into a crime scene. What would the potential ramifications have been? Contracted buyers might opt out of their deals. Development would shut down for the duration of the investigation. The bad press alone would be crippling, but adding unforeseen delays could cost them thousands of dollars per day. Hell, the developer probably had to shell out somewhere in the neighborhood of five million dollars for the land alone, then add to it the cost of the supplies and manpower, and the dwindling sales, and that was a recipe for financial ruin.

"Garnet Construction," he read aloud from the billboard-sized advertisement that showed an artist's conception of one of the finished homes beside the lake, with a paved walkway and a gazebo. Garnet was a local construction company, not some large corporation. They'd probably leveraged themselves to the hilt to finance the entire project. There weren't signs for any other construction companies, and there was only one dirty white trailer set up as a hub in the center of the construction.

He studied the dynamics for a while, watching as clusters of immigrant workers separated into three distinct groups. The smallest group dug the foundations, while the other two groups were equally divided into those who framed the skeletal houses and those who finished the project from there. His mere presence in their midst would be enough to intimidate the undoubtedly illegal workers, but they weren't the ones he wanted to talk to. He had a hunch that he needed to lean on whomever owned the brand new Cadillac sitting outside the trailer, beside a Ford pickup. That sedan was so out of place that it stood out like a beacon.

Darren pulled out from behind the willow blind and turned slowly down the street. He didn't even need to flash the siren lights so long as he drove slowly enough that it appeared as though he were looking for something specific. Eyes watched him from beneath hardhats and sweaty brows before vanishing deeper into the houses and out of sight. The laborers wanted nothing to do with a policeman, which in itself was nothing out of the ordinary. In his experience, they would aggregate into small clusters and watch him pass as though they could hide in their own numbers. The only time an illegal completely avoided confrontation was when he had good reason to do so.

By the time Darren reached the end of the gravel road, there wasn't a single worker visible in his rearview mirror. All of the tractors and caterpillars sat lifeless where their drivers had simply abandoned them.

"Interesting," he said. He parked parallel to the trailer so that he completely blocked the Cadillac from backing out. The oversized Ford pickup would have made short work of his cruiser regardless, so there was really no point in trying anything more ambitious than taking down the license plate number. He debated calling in his location, but this was only going to take a couple of minutes, and he was quite confident he'd be able to gauge their involvement by their expressions the moment he walked through the door into the trailer. It would be easy enough to get a warrant and come back later, but for now he just needed to follow up on a hunch.

Climbing out, he adjusted his utility belt and looked up into the early morning sun to feign nonchalance, in case they had already been alerted to his arrival. He stared back down the street, but none of the laborers had ventured back out from wherever they had gone. It was as though they were building a ghost town.

Darren walked between the two cars toward the building, running his palm over the enormous tires on the truck to the right, noting how there wasn't any dirt packed into the tread. Even the bed looked like it had recently received a good scrubbing. The ground around it was still wet, and though it had rained nearly the entire night, the area immediately surrounding the truck was far more damp than the rest of the area, with puddles standing in the small divots. Keeping his eyes on the door at the top of the small set of wooden stairs directly ahead, he ran his hand over the front tire. It was clean and damp as well.

There was certainly no law against washing one's car, but the circumstances surrounding it didn't sit well with Darren. Something was amiss here, and he had a good idea that his suspicions had been right on the money.

He looked back at the cruiser one final time and again debated calling it in to the station, but instead turned around, raised his right fist, and banged on the hollow-sounding door.

II

The silence had been their first clue. It wasn't as though all sounds of construction had ceased at once, but rather one at a time, dimming steadily until the last tractor engine stilled. There was no rapid pop of nail guns or grumble of aging motors, no banging of hammers or beeping of reversing earthmovers. No loud music or chatter over it. All of that could easily be tuned out to blend in with the background static that one barely noticed anymore after years in construction, but it was immediately recognizable when it stopped.

"What's going on out there?" Stan huffed, striding from the desk to the small window. He had just raised his hand to part the horizontal blinds when Jim grabbed him by the wrist.

"Sit down, Stan," Jim said. He locked eyes with his boss for a moment before he relaxed his grip.

Stan walked across the office and around the desk, already popping four pink Rolaids, crunching loudly. He slid the chair back with the screech of metal drawn across chipped linoleum, sat down, and tugged up his slacks just far enough so as not to threaten the crease.

"You had to know it was only a matter of time," Jim said. His right foot was crossed over his left on the edge of the desk, dirt crumbling from the soles onto the blotter. He leaned back in the chair and laced his fingers behind his head. With a content smile on his face, he didn't look like he had a care in the world.

Stan, on the other hand, grimaced against the stabbing pain in his gut. His bruised-looking eyes reflected the fact that he hadn't slept at all, and his jittery fingers tapped the desk at the urging of the copious amounts of caffeine in his bloodstream.

"I didn't figure it would be the next morning," he nearly shouted, before quickly modifying his tone. "What are we supposed to do now?"

"Get a hold of yourself, Stan. If they had any kind of proof, they would have been over here long before now. And they would have come flying in with their sirens on. I heard a grand total of one car. One, Stan. They're only trolling here."

There was the groan of applied weight on the first step outside, rocking the trailer ever so gently, before the second step creaked to betray their visitor.

"Are you sure?" Stan asked, nervously looking at the front door as it shivered against the force of the knocking.

"Would you just relax?" Jim said. He lowered his feet from the table and walked toward the front door. "What's the worst that could happen?"

III

"Officer Drury," Darren said, flashing his badge at the man who opened the door. "Would you mind if I came in and asked you a couple of questions?"

"Not at all," the man said. He opened the door wider and stepped out of Darren's way. "All of our permits are in order."

"I'm sure they are, Mister…"

"Savage," the man said, offering his right hand. "Jim Savage. Foreman."

The man had a strong grip, his skin callused and rough. There were no crescents of dirt beneath his fingernails, and his flannel shirt and faded jeans were heavily worn, but still clean. Darren didn't imagine that this was too far out of the ordinary for this early in the morning, but this wasn't the man he had come to see. He followed the scent of cologne and money to where another man sat behind a desk, wearing a buff-colored shirt with a blue silk tie, his suit jacket draped over the back of the chair. When Darren caught his eye, the man quickly averted his eyes, rose to his feet, and thrust his hand across the desk.

"Stan Garnet," the man said, briskly shaking Darren's hand. His smooth palm was damp, though not nearly to the same degree as his armpits, where there were oblong stains in the fabric. His irises twitched, but he managed to hold eye contact this time.

"Of Garnet Construction," Darren said. "I saw the sign on the way in. Looks like you've got a heck of an operation out here, Mr. Garnet, though at this rate it looks as though you may never get done."

Jim laughed. "They're like cockroaches. At the first sign of light they're gone to Lord only knows where, but I tell you, when they're out there working, there isn't anyone on this planet willing to work half as hard as those Mexicans."

"All completely legal, I would imagine."

"I have a stack of photocopied social security numbers to prove it," Jim said. "You want me to go grab—?"

"No, no," Darren said, stopping the foreman in his tracks, halfway out of the office and toward the adjoining room, which appeared to house little more than blueprints and a handful of file cabinets. "Everyone's entitled to earn a living."

"Then what *can* we do for you, Officer?"

Darren stepped farther into the room, removed his hat, held it across his chest. His sable-brown hair stood up on the left and lay straight back on the right, having dried that way beneath his cap and the slicker hood.

"I don't suppose either of you noticed all the police down at the lake on your way in this morning?" He looked first at Stan, who gave him precisely the reaction he had expected. The man looked like he'd just been punched in the gut, though he still wore the same awkward, crooked smile beneath his bushy mustache on his now pale face. His hand rested on his stomach like Napoleon's.

"Now that you mention it," Jim said, drawing Darren's attention, "I did notice a couple of cop cars down at the end of the road. I didn't think much of it at the time. It's not like you guys don't set up speed traps out here all the time."

Darren smiled and studied Jim a moment longer before turning back to Stan. "What do you think they found, Mr. Garnet?"

Garnet glanced to Darren's right, at Jim.

"I can't imagine, Officer," Stan said, swallowing very slowly and deliberately.

Darren smiled as Garnet squirmed beneath his scrutiny.

"Looks like someone went joyriding through the marsh," Darren finally said. The look of relief on Garnet's face was instantaneous, as was the sudden exhalation of the breath he'd apparently held too long. "Tore up the cattails pretty good. Even looks like they may have driven right out into the lake."

"How does that pertain to us?" Jim asked. He stepped in front of the desk so that Darren now had to look at him instead.

"Well, Mr. Savage, I don't suppose it does directly. I was just wondering if you guys might have seen anything out of the ordinary or noticed if anyone had been messing around on your site during the night."

"There are always kids leaving beer cans and whatnot in the houses, but I can't say there was anything that stands out from last night," Jim said, leveling his stare to meet Darren's. "Of course, we haven't been in all that long and haven't even had a chance to get out of this office at all yet."

"I'm sure you guys have so much to keep track of that you don't have time to constantly look for vandals."

"That's the truth," Jim said, crossing his arms over his chest.

"I can imagine." Darren forced a dry laugh. "You guys must have a pretty tight schedule to keep."

Jim cocked his head, but this time only responded with a nod and a grunt.

"Believe me, I understand. People expect us to drop everything and rush over to their house every time their dog wanders off or one of their kids is a little late for their curfew. Heaven forbid we're not immediately available every time someone finds a coyote bone and suspects a murder."

He smiled.

Jim looked back at him with hard, unflinching blue eyes.

"Oh, well," Darren said with a sigh. "I suppose since you guys have so much to do I could always just poke around a little on my way out. You know, see if the vandals did any damage to your property."

"That's a nice offer—" Jim started, but Darren cut him off.

"No trouble at all. I'm already all the way out here, right?" He turned, walked toward the door, and grasped the handle. He paused and spoke without looking back over his shoulder. "Don't worry, I'll be sure to let you know if I find anything."

"We'd certainly appreciate it," Jim said.

"Oh yeah, Mr. Garnet?" Darren stopped in the open doorway and looked back at the sweaty man behind the desk. "That your Caddie out there?"

Stan just nodded.

"Must be nice. I've always wanted a car like that. My grandfather used to have one back when I was a kid. Kept that thing in mint condition. A fly couldn't land on it without my grandfather knowing."

"It gets me from here to there," Stan said, unsticking his tongue from the roof of his mouth.

"In style, too, I'd bet. Thing is, those Cadillacs don't

mean the same thing they once did."

"How so?" Stan asked as Jim settled back into the chair in front of the desk.

"I can't imagine that in my grandfather's day anyone would have gone to all the effort of washing a pickup truck, but not the Caddie parked right beside it."

Stan's eyes grew wide in the silence that fell between them.

"You guys have a good rest of the morning," Darren said, and closed the door.

IV

Darren strode right between the two cars, tracing a knuckle through the dirt on the side of the Catera. He smiled to himself. That must have gotten under their skin. What could he do about it, anyway? Surely he could match the tire tread on the foreman's truck to those leading into Kettner Lake, but chances were it was a common size and model that belonged to a million other nearly identical vehicles. And even if he were able to positively match the tracks, without fingerprints on the bones, it would be all but impossible to pin it on them. It's not like he could really charge them with much of anything either. Disturbing the scene of a crime? He guessed Garnet had the kind of influence that could make that charge go away in a heartbeat, anyway. They'd relocated skeletal remains in the middle of a lake where two teenagers were suspected to have drowned sixteen years prior. Unless he was going to try to put together a case for murder, pursuing Garnet and the foreman would be a waste of time. Besides, they'd already told him what he needed to know. Maybe not in so many words, but judging by their reactions, his theory had been right on the money. Now he just needed to figure out where the bones had been unearthed, so he could get down to the real issue: putting together the pieces of a brutal crime that had happened more than half his lifetime ago.

Had he not still been within sight of the trailer, he might have laughed out loud. That had been way too much fun.

"So what do we know?" he whispered to himself as he passed his squad car. Even though the men knew that he was onto them, there was no point in baiting them any further. He had to make his search look lackadaisical, as though he were just going through the motions.

Based on the freshness of the tire tracks, the bones had only recently been relocated. He couldn't imagine that they could have dug up the bodies a long time ago and had just waited until now to dispose of them. They'd been hastily discarded, not planted. There had been no serious thought put into the process. The entire setup positively screamed that it had been a rush job. That must have meant that the skeletons had just been discovered, which narrowed his search to the half-dozen or so freshly dug foundations surrounding him. One of the crew must have come across them first. That's why they had all scurried off when they saw his cruiser, which only confirmed his assertion.

There was a cul-de-sac off to his left, the freshly leveled ground interrupted only by the enormous mounds of soil carved from the deep trenches, above which they stood like tombstones. The only distinguishing markers were plywood signs staked to two-by-fours, the proposed house numbers spray-painted onto the weathered surface. The electricity was still at the street, and they had yet to run the plumbing. He could imagine that the ground hadn't even been broken a week ago.

He walked to the edge of the first hole, braced his hands on his knees, and peered down. The metal frames for the footers were already in place, outlining the exact dimensions of the basement walls, but the cement had yet to be poured. To the right, the earth sloped upward, away from the hole. It was riddled with the marks of tractor treads and work boots. Darren scanned every earthen wall, looking for even the most minor imperfection, and scrutinized the ground for anything out of the ordinary. He even inspected the pile of dirt excavated from the earth for any sign that it had been disrupted in any fashion.

Shaking his head, he walked toward the second hole, farther down the road. What was he hoping to find anyway? If the skeletons had been scooped out of the ground in the middle of the hole and then discovered as soon as the load was dumped, the most he could hope to find were a few misplaced teeth or random missing carpals packed in the dirt. And that was after sifting carefully through each of the piles. It wasn't like he was going to discover—

Darren stopped at the rim of the second hole and stared down. A section of the wall had collapsed nearly right beneath his feet. It looked as though someone had hurriedly tried to pack it back into place, but the rain had washed away their efforts. Now it was merely a pile of mud down at the bottom of the cut with tire tracks leading right up to it.

He smiled to himself.

A couple steps to the right, and he dropped onto the slanted drive that angled down, into the foundation. He walked toward a crater in the formerly smooth dirt wall, mud accumulating on his heels, thickening and adding weight with each step. He glanced over the opposite rim of the hole to gauge his location in relation to the lake, which was about a hundred and fifty yards through the stands of cottonwoods and willows, and the flooded marsh beyond.

At the bottom of the ramp he took a mental snapshot, trying to engrave his first impression into his mind. He was just going to take a quick look around and then head back to the cruiser to call in his discovery.

The top of the crumbled section was two feet below the leveled surface, and extended all the way to the bottom of the hole. It was roughly four feet in diameter. At its deepest point, Darren could shove his arm in past the elbow. Assuming both of the bodies had been found here together, he could only imagine that they had been shoved down into some sort of vertical chute, one on top of the other. It wasn't deep enough for either of them to have been standing erect, nor wide enough for them to have been buried lying down. They must have been folded in half and shoved down into the ground, or worse, discarded in the impromptu grave part by part.

Something caught his eye in the dirt directly ahead of him. It looked like a rock, but as he gently brushed the packed dirt away from it, he exposed a longer section consistent in size and shape with one of the tarsals in the foot.

"Bingo," he whispered. He didn't dare brush away any more dirt for fear the bone would fall to the ground. The site needed to be left as undisturbed as possible. Even his muddy footprints were now regrettable.

There was a flash of light and then excruciating pain in the back of his head. He tasted blood in his mouth and sinuses. White stars expanded in his vision until they completely eclipsed the ground as it rushed toward his face.

V

Stan stood over the cop's body, and stared along the length of the wooden handle to the spaded end of the shovel. Blood drained in ribbons down toward his clenched fists. He started to tremble, dropped the shovel, and backed away from the man who was now crumpled against the base of the earthen wall.

He tasted blood and hurriedly pried his hands from where he'd clasped them over his mouth in shock. His cheeks were freckled with droplets of crimson. Staggering backward, he tripped over his own feet and fell in the mud.

"I just… He was going to…" Stan stammered. He shook his head. "They would have shut us down."

"Snap out of it," Jim said, grabbing Stan by twin handfuls of shirt and hauling him to his feet. "Be a man for once in your miserable life."

Stan looked at Jim through impossibly wide eyes, unable to comprehend a single word the larger man was saying, then back down to the ground. Blood flowed freely from the back of the officer's head, running down his neck and soaked into his now black uniform. White fragments of bone poked through the tatters of mangled scalp and hair.

"Stan!" Jim slapped him right across the face. A furious red welt rose on Stan's stubbled cheek as he turned to look at Jim. His pupils grew wide and then shrunk to pinpricks before finally settling somewhere in between. A measure of sentience returned to his eyes.

"We're going to need to get the body out of here without anyone seeing it," Stan said. He straightened his tie with muddied hands that left smears all over his dress shirt. "And we'll need to get rid of his car."

Jim nodded solemnly and took a step back.

"Any witnesses?" Stan asked, turning on unsteady legs to look up the slant.

"They're all too scared of being deported to be anywhere near the cop."

Stan nodded. His eyes had resumed their normal size, and the color had returned to his face.

"We're going to need to get him out of his clothes," Stan said, rolling up his sleeves. He knelt on the ground beside the crumpled body and rolled it onto its back so that he could begin unbuttoning the shirt.

Jim slowly nodded his understanding, and started undoing the buttons down the front of his own flannel shirt.

CHAPTER 11

STRINGS

I

"Are you absolutely sure you saw the same thing I did?" Steve asked.

They were sitting on folding chairs beneath the overhang in Teri's back yard. It hadn't felt right inviting two complete strangers she had met in the middle of the night at a crime scene into her house, but she wasn't prepared to be alone yet either. Fortunately, the morning was nice enough that she was able to serve them steaming mugs of coffee on the patio, the rising sun reflecting off the lake in the distance.

"Without being able to see through your eyes, I can't be one hundred percent sure, but it does sound like we're talking about the same person," Teri said. She leaned back in the chair and stroked Bo's head.

Starlings chattered at they darted from the tops of the cattails, flashing the red of breeding season on their wings.

"It's certainly not an uncommon delusion," Kevin said. He took a long sip from the hot mug. "The human mind is far more powerful than we've even begun to comprehend."

"How could we both be making up the same thing?" Steve nearly shouted. He closed his eyes and took a deep breath. "Sorry. I didn't mean to jump on you."

Kevin waved off his apology.

"It's been a long night, and we're all tired. You're entitled."

Steve nodded. His name badge had broken off its clip, leaving only a blue lanyard hanging around his neck. His scrub top was resplendent with mud, the shirt beneath still damp from the mixture of sweat and rain.

"Let's break the situation down to the lowest common denominator," Kevin said, gesturing with his hands as he spoke. "Steve. You say you saw this figure in a black cloak on the night your brother died. While Teri, you say you saw this manifestation after allegedly witnessing a young girl's murder in the sewer. What do both of these scenarios have in common? Death."

He took another sip of the coffee and appeared to savor it for a moment before he continued.

"Death has been personified as many things through the course of history, the most common of which is now the Grim Reaper, whom both of you have described. The black cloak. The sickle. Claiming the bodies of the dead. It all makes sense.

"The brain has many defense mechanisms to prevent permanent psychological damage and to rationalize events in a way that won't traumatize the mind. People desperate for something to believe in will see The Virgin Mary in everything from their toast to the reflections cast from windows. To them, these illusions are the spitting image of the Holy Mother because that's how they choose to see them—whether consciously or not. In actuality though, they're nothing more than the random patterns of baked dough in the center of a loaf or a simple refraction of light from glass.

"My assertion is that you both witnessed something beyond your immediate comprehension, so to spare you from the extreme emotional trauma, your minds rationalized what you saw into something that you both readily recognized and accepted as a symbol of what you were witnessing. In essence, your minds transformed the images of death into the image of Death."

Kevin leaned back and drank contentedly from his mug.

"How much do we owe you for that psychoanalysis?" Steve asked.

"Oh, nothing. I was just…" Kevin noticed the expression on Steve's face. "I see. You were being facetious."

"No, that was just your mind rationalizing what I said into something you'd have an easier time dealing with."

"Guys," Teri said, sighing. While she could appreciate the logic behind what Kevin was saying, every part of her being screamed that what she had seen was real, not some figment of her imagination. "Arguing isn't going to get us anywhere."

"What do you propose then?" Steve asked.

"Okay…" Teri nibbled her lower lip as she stood. She set her mug down on the chair and paced from one end of the patio to the other while she talked. "Let's look at it from a different perspective. Say we both saw exactly what we claim we saw. Say there actually was a man—"

"Which there was," Steve interjected.

"Let her finish," Kevin said.

"Are you through?" she demanded. "We're all on edge, and our tempers are short. We can either get through this or we can let it go. And while the second option sounds far more appealing to me, I really don't think I can."

The men stared at her as she repeatedly blinked to stall the tears.

"Let me try again," she said. "Just for argument's sake, let's say that what we both saw was real, that we don't share some sort of group psychosis, and that there's some man out there dressed in black, carrying a sickle like the Grim Reaper. I know how that sounds…but I also know what I saw. Let's take a logical approach. How long ago was it that you saw him?"

"Sixteen years," Steve said.

"Say there's someone who's been killing people out here for the last sixteen years, some sort of serial killer. We have two of the three bodies as evidence, the blood in the sewer, and two eye-witnesses. The only thing we don't actually have is a suspect."

"That's the police's job," Kevin said.

"And a fine job they've done so far," Steve said. "How many suspects have they rounded up in the last decade and a half, hmm?"

"That's not the point."

"Of course that's the point!"

"Guys!" Teri snapped. "Would you quit arguing long enough for me to run with this line of thought?"

Kevin stripped his tie from around his neck, wadded it up, and shoved it into the pocket of his drenched jacket. With a single nod of agreement, he unbuttoned the top two buttons and looked at Steve.

"You know that I of all people understand what you've gone through during the last sixteen years," he said.

"They found your brother's body," Steve said. He unconsciously wrung his hands in his lap. "You have no idea what I've gone through."

"Do you think having a body makes it any easier? Do you think I don't still see my brother's blood pooling on the garage floor every time I close my eyes? Kyle didn't kill himself. Not the way I see it. Whatever happened out here that night killed him. I *need* to know what happened. I need to know… why."

Steve looked up from his lap and met Kevin's stare. The red faded from his cheeks, and he nodded slowly.

"Back to the facts," Teri said. She sat back down and nervously tapped her feet. "I've been going over and over this in my head. I could clearly see this man, but only when there was lightning. Granted, it was dark, but I can't believe it was so dark that I couldn't see him at all in the interim."

"I noticed the same thing," Steve said. "There was one point where he was right behind us—he was so close that I could feel the wind from his blade when he swung it—and then he was gone. It wasn't that we couldn't see him. He was literally no longer there. But when the lightning struck again, he was right there, only we'd been given enough time to get farther away from him."

"So, taken at face value, we can assume that this man exists only during a lightning strike, but doesn't exist at all in the time between strikes," Teri said.

"That's absurd," Kevin said, but then recanted with a curt nod and gestured for her to proceed.

"What do we know about lightning?" she asked. "It's only present during a thunderstorm, not just with precipitation, as it doesn't strike during a snowstorm. Lightning itself is a stream of negative electrons discharged from two clouds in an effort to balance the static charge between them, using the earth as something of a ground."

"Electrons moving at the speed of light are converted to photons, which are essentially bundles of energy with no mass, but a ton of potential," Steve said.

"Which creates an electrical current that flows between the earth and the atmosphere in an effort to reestablish the balance between positive and negative charges, since there must always be an equal amount of both. What then do we know about photons traveling at the speed of light?"

"They're subject to the same rules as any other

particle in motion. They have a wavelength that is inversely proportional to their frequency."

"Right. And as lightning is within the visible range of light, these photons will fall onto the electromagnetic spectrum toward the top of the energy scale," Teri paused and looked out across the lake, trying to focus her thoughts. "High energy photons are capable of producing electrostatic events as they interact with the molecules in the air. They disturb the balance between the positively charged protons and the negatively charged electrons in an atom enough to potentially create a phenomenon known as electron spin."

Teri scrunched her brow and rose to her feet. She looked first at Steve and then at Kevin. Her stare finally settled somewhere between.

"Are you all right?" Kevin asked.

"They say that mythology is a collection of fabrications based on events that really happened. Stories made up to rationalize events that the people of the time couldn't explain. The story of Noah's Ark grew from the verifiable flooding of the Tigris and Euphrates Rivers. Legends of dragons arose from the discovery of dinosaur bones."

She moved her hands as though trying to coax the next logical leap from them.

"The Grim Reaper," she said.

"How could the Grim Reaper possibly be real?" Kevin asked.

Teri smiled.

"Strings."

II

"I've studied the theory behind String Theory." Teri looked along the back of her house while her lower lip slipped between her teeth. Without a word, she stepped from the patio and onto the dirt. She grabbed the end of the rolled hose she was hoping to use soon to water her grass seed, walked back to the porch, and dropped it on the ground between Kevin and Steve. "It's a theoretical physicist's wet dream. A marriage of Quantum Field Theory and Einstein's Theory of General Relativity, quite possibly the missing link in the unified field model of physics. Imagine that the world, everything for that matter, doesn't just exist in the standard three dimensions we can perceive. We already know that there's a fourth dimension—"

"Time," Kevin said.

"Exactly. So we have a three-dimensional object that we can track through the fourth dimension of time. That covers everything we can physically observe. Now, String Theory instead proposes that there are not just those four dimensions, but rather ten, or possibly even more."

"How?"

"Look." She picked up the garden hose and stretched it between her fists until it was taut. She held it up to them so that it was parallel to her chest. "This hose is clearly a three-dimensional object. It has thickness, length, and height. As you look at it from my left hand toward my right in increments, it also exists over time. Now check this out."

She turned the hose so that they could both clearly see through the opening and into the rubber tube. Had it been attached to a spigot, they'd have both been drenched.

"What am I looking at?" Steve asked. "It's just a hose like any other."

"Think about it. We've already established the first four dimensions looking at it from the side. Thickness, length, height, and time. Consider the possibility that a fifth dimension can exist inside of the other four without being clearly visible." She pulled the hose tight again and held it up to Kevin. "Now pluck it like a guitar string."

He reached out and tapped the hose, causing it to shiver briefly between her hands.

"Did you see how the hose vibrated? You could see the uppermost limits of the vibration and the lowermost at the same time, and the true hose somewhere between, almost like a blur above and below. The hose isn't in those three different places at once, since it's simply a single three-dimensional object, but you could argue that if the hose were vibrating fast enough, it could be in those three different places at the exact same time, since you could actually see it. It would just be moving so fast that at any micro-moment in time, any single snapshot, it wouldn't be physically moving at all, but rather just in a different place than it would be a fraction of a second earlier or later. In that one point in time, the hose exists in a completely different dimension. Simply put, in one heartbeat it's there and in the next it's not. It still physically exists in a slightly altered location, but at that particular moment, it no longer exists in the same four dimensions that it did a moment prior."

"But what does any of this have to do with the lightning?" Steve asked.

"Can't you see? The lightning plucks the string, or the hose, for the sake of this example."

She hopped up and down in frustration. How was it that they weren't following her through this? It all made complete theoretical sense in her head.

"Okay," she said. She took a deep breath and tried to simplify it as much as she possibly could. "The air around us is packed with molecules: oxygen, carbon dioxide, whatnot. Each of these molecules contains a stable number of electrons in the outermost valence shell of its atomic structure. These molecules are just floating out there, minding their own business, when all of a sudden the lightning strikes. This big bolt of negative electrons tears right through their midst, and attracts the positive charges in the nucleus of these atoms while it simultaneously repels the negative charges in the orbital shells. It would be like two magnets trying to fight through their own opposing charges to stick together, even though they can't. So what does that do? It causes the entire molecule to spin, not just in one dimension like a top, but in multiple and unpredictable dimensions at the same time, like the hose. If they all turn just right, you can see straight through them, in a manner of speaking, just like looking into the hose."

"You're saying the lightning causes some sort of rift in the space-time continuum," Kevin said. "If that were the case, then why would this phenomenon only happen here and not everywhere else in the world during the thousands of thunderstorms every day?"

"I don't know. The air around us isn't of uniform molecular composition. More plants change the nitrogen composition. Lakes like this one produce varying amounts of gasses like methane. Even the radiation caused by the sun's rays is different at every altitude. Maybe it so happens that the combination we have here is just right, so that the lightning acts as a catalyst, and causes just enough of a shift in the molecular arrangement surrounding us to allow not just a glimpse into another dimension, but an actual doorway between the two."

III

"So, in essence, you're suggesting is that there's a real Grim Reaper that exists in a parallel dimension, who's able to escape during lightning strikes," Kevin said. He stood and patted his pocket to make sure his car keys were still there. "But we ruled out the prospect of a serial killer because that was just too unlikely?" He chuckled. "I'm heading home. I could really use some sleep, and it sounds to me like you guys could as well."

"There's only one way to find out if you're right," Steve said, looking to Teri.

"I haven't heard the forecast. Is it supposed to rain again?" she asked.

"I don't know," Steve said with a shrug. "We've been getting these storms just about every afternoon for the last couple of weeks, but I don't think I have that kind of patience."

"I suppose now you can make it rain," Kevin said.

"I thought you were leaving," Steve said.

"Now you've piqued my curiosity. Are you going to do some kind of rain dance or seed the clouds? Look!" He threw up his arms and spun in a circle. "Not a cloud in the sky."

Steve shook his head. "Since all photons travel at the speed of light, I don't suppose it would matter where a stream of electrons originated, so long as the wavelength and frequency were similar, would it?"

"Not in theory," Teri said, her brow lowered in contemplation. She unconsciously chewed on her lower lip. "But where would we be able to find a source capable of producing that much energy?"

Steve smiled.

"Leave that to me."

CHAPTER 12

ELECTROMAGNETIC SPECTRUM

I

Steve sneaked into the hospital through the service entrance. He'd walked out in the middle of his shift, and he could only imagine the ramifications. Eventually, he'd have to deal with his boss, but now wasn't the time. He was in no mood for confrontation. Whatever may come of it, he'd deal with the consequences some other time.

Besides, he was about to do something far worse.

He crept up the back stairs by the service elevator, to the second floor, and peered at the hallway beyond through the mesh-reinforced glass set in the heavy door. It was empty, as he had been sure it would be. There were no offices down this corridor, only supply closets for each of the departments, an electrical room, and a janitorial closet.

Silently, he turned the knob and pushed the door open. He eased through and gently closed the door behind him, so as not to make even the faintest click. Keeping his right shoulder against the white-paneled wall, he crept down to the T-intersection at the end of the hallway. There was a rounded mirror positioned directly ahead, between the wall and the ceiling like a spider web, and though it dramatically distorted everything it reflected, he could see all the way down the hallway to either side.

This was the juncture where speed became of the essence.

He turned right and walked quickly down the hallway until he came to a twin bank of elevators that led either up to nephrology or down to the ICU. Sitting beside them was a line of three portable x-ray machines. They'd notice immediately if he took the newest one that all of the technologists liked to use, but since no one ever used the oldest machine, it would probably take the department quite a while to miss it. Unlike the more modern equipment, the old style gave him control not just over kilovoltage and milliamperes, but it gave him a separate time dial that he could crank all the way up to two seconds. Granted, that wasn't very long, but it would have to work.

Unplugging it from the wall, he turned the power knob and waited for a long moment while the battery unit switched over from the charge setting. Grasping the handle tightly in both hands, he backed it in reverse to get it away from the wall and then turned it back in the direction from which he'd come. Progress was maddeningly slow, as the older unit didn't have much oomph when it came to self-propulsion, but eventually he reached the service elevator next to the staircase and pressed the down button.

Left foot tapping nervously, he looked back down the hallway, expecting someone to come rushing around the corner at any second. He could hear the grinding and clanking of the elevator car as it rose from the bottom level and settled with a solid thump in front of the machine. The doors parted with an audible whine, and he drove the unit inside.

It wasn't until the doors closed in front of him that he let out the breath he'd been holding.

The floor came to rest beneath him, and the number one lit up above the closed doors with a ding. As the doors opened, Steve leaned just far enough out to look down the hallway. He was already backing the unit out of the elevator by the time it registered that there had been a janitor's cart twenty feet down the corridor that hadn't been there before, but there had been no one with it. Continuing in reverse, he thrust his rear end against the push-handle of the outside door and threw it open into a small cove.

Industrial-sized dumpsters lined the brick wall to the left, their contents reeking of hospital food long since turned, while against the right wall was an enormous bin overflowing with large red bags of soiled laundry. The U-Haul truck he had rented was backed right in between, with the loading ramp extended, leading up into the open cargo area, just as he had left it.

He guided the portable machine straight up the grooved ramp, which made a buzzing sound like a playing card against bike spokes, until he reached the top and pushed it clear to the front of the empty hold. Racing back outside, he lifted the ramp and shoved it back beneath the truck with a loud bang, then leapt onto the fender, grabbed the handle, and brought the door down until he was able to latch it closed.

Steve sprinted around the side of the truck and threw open the driver's side door. He leapt up, cranked the ignition, and stomped on the gas pedal.

"Come on, come on."

The engine came to life with a roar and a tuft of black smoke from beneath the hood. He put it in gear, and the truck lurched forward. With a sigh of relief, he turned out into the employee parking lot and headed for the main road.

II

He'd been surprised to find Kevin's car parked in front of Teri's house when he returned with the truck. For all of the shrink's grousing, maybe there was a small part of him that at least wanted to believe there was something to Teri's theory. Steve didn't even know if *he* believed, for that matter, but he would do just about anything to find out what had happened to Brian all those years ago. The image he'd seen on the x-ray—of his brother in so much pain—haunted him.

"How much farther?" Teri asked. She walked in front of them along the path, holding the dog's leash in one hand and a digital camera in the other.

Steve looked up from where he crouched to the stand of trees he remembered so well from that night.

"Just up the path in the middle of those trees," he said.

They had borrowed four two-by-fours from one of the construction sites to use almost like train rails. There was no way they were going to be able to push the heavy portable x-ray machine through the marsh on those tiny wheels, even with the minimal self-propulsion. So they'd driven it down as far as possible in the U-Haul, and now were maneuvering the unit precariously forward, down the swampy path, on the parallel lengths of wood, balancing the wheels just well enough to reach the end of those rails while the others placed two more long boards in front of the last set. After the cart had been pushed onto the next set of planks, they would head back around behind the portable unit, pry the last set of wooden rails from the mire, take them back around to the front, and lay them at the end of the track.

The midday heat was unbearable, and both Kevin and Steve were covered with sweat and swamp water, their own odors indecipherable from the various gasses burbling from the marsh.

By the time they reached the point where the path was swallowed by a mouth of willow branches, both men were on the verge of collapsing. Bending and standing repeatedly had taken its toll on their thighs, making it feel as though invisible fire blazed beneath the skin. As Steve remembered, the path rose out of the marsh and onto higher ground, where they'd be able to guide the cart without using those infernal rails. His heart was beating so fast in anticipation that his breathing bordered on hyperventilation. He didn't know what they would find in there, if anything. Perhaps all they would discover was that they had wasted their time and energy driving the machine out there through the reeds, that Steve had risked his job and a potential criminal record for nothing. Or maybe, just maybe, they would find exactly what they were looking for.

"Is this it?" Teri asked. She hesitated and rubbed the goose bumps that had risen on her arms. An aura of coldness radiated from the other side of the willows.

Bo whimpered and sat behind her on the path, floppy ears folded all the way back.

"Yeah," Steve said, standing fully erect and bracing his sore back. He wiped the sweat from his brow with his shirt sleeve. "That's it for sure."

"Then what are we waiting for?" Kevin asked, finally guiding the machine over the end of the wooden planks and onto solid ground.

"Can't you feel it?" Teri whispered. She stared through the fluttering leaves dancing gently on the breeze, into the shadows beyond.

"Feel what?" Kevin asked, but he knew exactly what she was talking about. It was as though fishing hooks made of ice had lanced down through his pores. He'd never experienced anything like it. His first impulse was to turn tail and sprint in the opposite direction, but this kind of physiological response triggered his professional curiosity. It was a physical improbability that the temperature would drop so dramatically from one step to the next, and the wind wasn't blowing any harder than it had been before.

There was something back there, in the shadows beneath the trees, simultaneously drawing them to it and pushing them away at the same time. It was as though the air itself was alive with electricity.

"Let's just get this done," Steve said, stepping behind the portable x-ray machine and squeezing the handle. He had to lower his center of gravity and shove, but he was able to drive it forward along the path, bending branches back and snapping those unable to. Spearhead-shaped leaves were torn from their moorings to litter the ground. The branches closed around him like so many hands trying to grab his shirt and hair, scratching at his face.

Ducking his head, he emerged from the tangled thicket, into the small clearing. It was different than he remembered, but the image he kept tucked away in his mind was of skinned squirrels hanging by nails through their tails, bones crunching underfoot and dangling from the trees like windchimes. This section of ground appeared bland by comparison.

He reached under his collar and drew out the long leather lace and the arrowhead affixed to the end of it. Clasping it tightly in his palm, he waited for the racket of trampling leaves and snapping twigs to cease as the others joined him within the enclave.

The last time he had been here was more than half his lifetime ago, and he remembered it through the eyes of a child. The ceiling of branches was much lower, forcing him to stoop just a little to keep from tearing open his scalp on one of the many sharp branches that still protruded from the amber-seething wood. Last time, he had been here after sundown, which had surely contributed to the overall sense of dread. Now, the ground was spotted with dime-sized circles of light that managed to pierce the upper canopy, highlighting a mat of decomposing leaves, bark, and fractured sticks on the ground. Sap was frozen on the face of each of the trees like oft-used candles, draining down one layer after another. A fresh wound bled from the bare pulp, the grain frayed as though a bear had used it to sharpen its claws.

It smelled of decomposition beneath the canopy, the leaves of summers past slowly working their way back into the earth from which they had sprung, mildewing in the trapped humidity.

"We'll only have two shots at this," Steve said. He raised the extendable armature from the top of the unit, and held it by the handles on either side of the light-projecting head.

"We dragged this thing all the way out here for two shots?" Kevin griped. "I thought you said each of these exposures would only last two seconds."

"Right."

"So we spent the last two hours pushing this enormous block of dead weight through the cattails for four seconds?"

Steve hated to think of it that way, but nodded in agreement.

"Don't mess up, then."

Steve tilted the head until it was parallel with the ground and pointed it at one of the large trunks where freshets of sap seeped from a deep gouge. He pressed the black button, which produced a stream of light. With a twist of each of the collimator knobs, he opened the light field as wide as he could, brightening the tree and the snarls of brush behind.

"Are you ready?" he asked, walking back around to the control panel.

"Yeah," Teri whispered. She dropped Bo's leash, and he darted back out along the path. Raising the camera, she focused on the large square of projected light.

Steve fiddled with the dials. He set the kilovoltage as high as it would go to generate the greatest power, the current at one hundred milliamperes, and then cranked the time knob all the way to the right until it indicated two seconds.

"Is everyone watching?" Steve asked, removing the handheld exposure button from its holster. He stretched it to the end of its coiled tether and gestured for the others to move back as well.

Teri's hands shook as she held the camera away from her body, using the digital viewing window on the back to align her shot.

"Shooting x-ray," Steve said out of habit, his voice cracking.

The machine made a whirring sound as he held down the rotor switch. He gently applied more and more pressure with his thumb until there was a loud *beep*.

III

The light blossoming from the head died when the exposure started. With the sudden advance of shadows, it took Teri's eyes a moment to adjust as the beep droned on beneath the canopy. Invisible tungsten electrons sped from the focal tract through the air. Her heart sunk, as at first she couldn't see anything at all, but when she pressed the button on the top of the camera and the flash went off, it was all she could do to keep from screaming.

In that one brief strobe of luminescence, the square where the x-rays were being directed stood open like a window. Everything around it appeared as it had a second prior, but through that square lay horrors beyond anything she'd ever seen. Where the fresh sap seeped from the pulp, there was a wide, rusted railroad spike. Five fingers framed it like the petals of a flower. The skin was a sickly shade of gray, the crescents at the base of the fingernails turning blue. Severed tendons and desiccated vessels dangled from the tatter of flesh where the wrist had once been. A bloody strap of skin was tied around the trunk above it, as though in the process of being stretched and tanned. Long bones were suspended from above by cords made of lashed reeds, twisting on the faint breeze.

The smell that assaulted her, as though blown through that open window, was more than she could bear. She clapped her hand over her mouth and looked away, retching as she tried to keep from vomiting.

The image lingered even after the flash died, though the atrocities seen through the window were swathed in darkness, masking all but the most vivid details. When the exposure terminated, stranding them again in silence, the world returned to normal directly in front of them, as though what they'd seen had never truly existed.

"Did you get that?" Kevin asked, looking to Teri with wide, panicked eyes.

She lowered the camera to where she had just enough light to decipher the buttons, and brought up the last image. It was all there, just as it had been during the irradiation. Her eyes snapped back up to look at the tree, where there were now only the thick streams of sap. She looked back down, and the image was still there. A hand with an iron spike through the middle of it, like an unseeing eye; bones dangling from somewhere above, casting long shadows back into the willows; and even things she hadn't noticed. A rabbit was staked to one of the overhead branches by a nail driven straight up through its jaw and out the top of its head into the wood. The remainder of the nail had been pounded sideways to pinch half of the head, so that it appeared to be squinting through vacuous sockets. A pair of long, flaccid rear limbs hung from beneath the gutted abdomen.

"Did you get it?" Kevin shouted.

Teri raised her head. All of the color had drained from her face. She could barely force a single nod.

"Let me see," Kevin said, grabbing the camera out of her hands and bringing it right up to his face. "Oh, God."

He averted his eyes and offered the camera to Steve, who shook his head. He'd clearly seen it already. Instead, he walked right up to the trunk and ran his palm along the smooth wood, where the bark had been shredded away, taking his time to prove to himself that his tactile senses weren't deceiving him, that there really was no hand staked to the tree where the sap bled from the wound.

"We've got one more exposure at the most…if we didn't drain too much of the battery trying to push it out here," he said, drawing his gooey hand back from the tree.

"We should pull it back farther so we can see a larger area," Teri said. She couldn't bring herself to even look in the general direction of where she had seen what she assumed to be the hand of the girl she had seen the night before, perhaps even the same hand she'd been unable to grasp well enough to save her.

"We should just get out of here," Kevin said, taking a couple steps in reverse and pressing his back against another trunk. He nearly jumped out of his skin in his hurry to get away from it.

"One more," Steve whispered. He walked over to Kevin and handed him the exposure trigger. "When I tell you, push softly on the button until you hear the purr of the rotor, then press the button all the way down and hold it down until the beep stops."

"Why do *I* have to do this?"

"Just do it when I tell you to, okay?" Steve returned to the front of the machine and pressed the button that summoned the square of light again. "Are you ready with the camera?"

"Just a second," Teri said, hurrying over to Kevin, who was already holding the Kodak out for her. She walked back over to where she'd been standing before and looked from Steve to Kevin. "Okay."

She held the camera up in front of her.

Steve took in a deep, stuttering breath.

"You're going to have to move one way or the other," Teri said. "You're right in the middle of the picture."

Steve tried to force a smile.

"Kevin," he said, turning his back to the machine. "Hit the button."

IV

"What are you doing?" Teri shouted over the whir of the spinning rotor, but Steve could hardly hear her. All of his concentration was focused on what was coming next.

"Now!" he yelled.

"Get away—!" Teri screamed, but her words were cut off by the high-pitched tone of the machine as it fired millions of accelerated x-rays right at Steve's back.

To Steve, it looked almost like he'd stepped in front of a projector in a theater, but instead of his head and shoulders completely eclipsing the scene, it was just substantially dulled, like a fog, as his body attenuated the majority of the radiation. The smell hit him squarely in the face like a baseball bat, nearly knocking him over. His head started to spin as a greasy stench drained down the back of his throat from his sinuses, tasting of blood and rot. He pulled his undershirt up over his mouth and nose with his left hand and reached out with his right. It felt like reaching through a picture frame into some hellish acrylic landscape. Even the air felt heavier, the humidity beading on the back of his arm as he watched his fanned fingers as if they were attached to someone else's body entirely. A cloud of mosquitoes arose from nowhere and swarmed around his arm, alighting on the skin in preparation of drawing blood.

His first instinct was to try to grab the hand nailed to the trunk, but he only had a single second left to work with, so he needed to make it count. If he tried for the hand and was unable to wrench it from the stake, he wouldn't get another shot at it. He had to be quick and decisive, so he grabbed for the closest thing to him: a long bone dangling by woven weeds from above. Part of him didn't think it would physically be there until his hand closed around it and he felt it, cold and smooth, the miniature imperfections pressing into his palm like wood grain. He jerked his arm back with every ounce of his strength. The resistance was more than he'd expected, as the hewn rope was not nearly as brittle as it looked. The tether abruptly snapped, and he fell backwards into the painfully silent clearing. Every ounce of juice had been sapped from the machine.

His rear end hammered the ground first, clattering his teeth together, and the back of his head rammed the front corner of the x-ray machine.

Stars exploded across his vision, already dotted with the starburst shapes of the sun reaching through the dense canopy.

He heard Teri screaming, and then she was upon him, turning his head to the left and lowering him onto the ground on his side. She cradled his head in her lap. Her bright red face stared down at him, tears welling in the corners of her eyes. Kevin eclipsed the light momentarily as he dropped to his knees, leaned over him, and shouted something that was unable to penetrate the ringing in his ears. His eyes slowly fell from Kevin toward the ground until they fixed upon his own extended right arm and the long shaft of age-browned bone projecting out from either side of his fist.

CHAPTER 13
THE COMING STORM

I

Stan stood at the end of the street, staring at the Rocky Mountains to the west. Black storm clouds crested the jagged peaks like burbling molasses boiling over the edge of a pot. The sun descended from above like a slow-motion cannonball. He peeled the wrapper from the last two Rolaids and threw it onto the ground, stomping on it out of frustration as he crunched the chalky discs. His stomach felt like whatever ulcer may have been there yesterday had yawned wide enough to let all of the acid out to attack his body. Sharp pains stabbed his abdomen, fire rose up his esophagus, and his bowels growled like so many starving wolves. It was the price one paid for success, he figured. As soon as this rotten chore was done, he could go back to his sixty-five-hundred square-foot house overlooking the city and relax beneath the stars with a snifter of cognac.

He imagined it was only a matter of time before someone started to miss the cop, if they hadn't already, so the sooner they disposed of the body, the better he'd feel. Jim hadn't come back from hiding the vehicle yet, and it had been close to nine hours already. His foreman was a perfectionist, which was half the reason he respected the man so much. If Jim put as much effort into ditching that vehicle as he did into each of the homes, no one would ever find it. His bigger worry was the body at the bottom of the foundation to his left. They'd left it there, after heaping mounds of dirt atop it, as neither could think of a reasonable way to get it out of the hole without drawing attention to themselves, at least not until the crew was dismissed for the day.

All of the workers had left promptly at four, those who'd been reassigned from the foundations to interior finishing thankful for the respite from another long day beneath the blazing sun.

He couldn't have sent them home early, as that would have aroused too much suspicion. He worked those laborers right up until the clock struck four. No one was a minute late arriving in the morning or coming back from lunch if they wanted to keep their jobs. Passing the afternoon, alone with his nerves and the thought of the body a couple hundred yards away, where someone could accidentally discover it at any moment, had been sheer torture. Each minute felt as though it stretched into an hour, each hour becoming an infinite test of his endurance. He'd sweated through his first shirt, and his second hadn't lasted much longer. Each time the phone had rung or a car had pulled into the development, he had thought that he was screwed. He had to continually remind himself that so long as the body was in his possession, there was no way anyone would suspect him. So he'd sat by the window in the office, peering through the slats in the horizontal blinds from just far enough away so as not to be overly conspicuous, watching the lot where they had killed the man—where *he* had killed the man—fearing even to blink.

Now that he was alone out there in the construction zone, clear across the lake from the finished residential area, he was finally able to breathe. By the time the sun set, this would all be over, and no one would ever find the body. Maybe one day they'd find the car, or whatever was left of it, and begin their investigation in earnest, but that gave him plenty of time to stow whatever minuscule amount of guilt might still linger and try to repress the entire deed.

So long as he was able to trust Jim, no one would ever know but the two of them. Jim had the cop's blood on his hands, too, so there was no way he was going to intentionally let that information slip.

Stan walked across the leveled front yard to the open hole, where one day a three-hundred thousand dollar house would stand. He stood at the lip of the cut, glancing down just long enough to verify the piles of dirt were still as he had left them, then looked out over the lake to the south, where the sun reflected off the tranquil water through the gaps in the trees.

The first distant rumble of thunder reached his ears from the storm that had now overtaken the mountains.

II

Stan saw Jim coming for the last half mile of the journey. He was on foot, though where he had appeared from, Stan had absolutely no idea. It was as though he had simply materialized from the transitional forests that slanted up into the foothills, where willows and aspens faded gently to pines and spruces. The roiling thunderheads grumbled ominously overhead as they stretched to the east, eclipsing the last of the sun's pristine rays.

"It's about time," Stan called to him as soon as Jim was within earshot. He'd meant it to sound flippant, but it came out razor-honed.

Jim didn't respond. He just walked right up beside Stan and looked down into the hole.

"I wanted to wait for you," Stan said.

"I can see that."

They stood in silence, neither of them particularly eager to begin the task, though both were anxious to get it over with.

"What did you do with the car?" Stan finally asked.

"Do you really want to know?"

"No," Stan whispered. "I don't suppose I do."

"No one will find it anytime soon. They may find the global tracking device in the middle of a lake as soon as they start to look for him, but they'll never find the rest of the car. I've seen to that."

"Thank you," Stan sighed. "I don't know what I'd do without you."

Jim, not one for sentiment, nodded and dropped down into the pit.

He rolled up the sleeves of the flannel shirt he'd changed into on his way back and grabbed the shovel, driving the point of the spade right into the loose dirt with a *snick*. Scattering the dirt as evenly as he could, Jim finally reachedthe nearly naked officer lying facedown, his white undershirt, boxers, and socks mottled a muddy brown.

"Well," Jim said, looking back up to the top of the hole, where Stan hadn't moved an inch. "Aren't you going to come down here and help?"

Stan looked like he was passing a stone, but he turned, regardless, and walked to the slope leading into the foundation.

"How do you want to do this?" Stan asked. The first raindrop tapped him on the shoulder as the storm flashed with blue lightning, now only miles to the west.

"Grab his legs."

Jim clasped the cop's wrists and raised them just far enough that he didn't have to stoop. The corpse's head flopped forward on its noodle neck.

"Wouldn't it be easier if we turned him over?"

"You want to look at his face, you go right ahead.

Me? I want nothing to do with it."

Stan dug his well-manicured fingers into the earth beneath the man's ankles, making sure to grab where there would be sock between his skin and the body's, and raised the feet, bending the legs at the knees.

"We need to pick up the pace," Jim said, looking back over his shoulder at the coming storm. They still had a couple hours before sunset, but the day was turning gray in a hurry.

"Where are we going?"

"Just lift the legs and follow me."

Stan heaved the long appendages up with a groan while Jim wrapped his arms around the man's chest beneath his arms, the head bent so sharply down that the back of his neck was against Jim's stomach. The body bowed awkwardly between them like an inverted rainbow as Stan juggled the legs to get a better grip, and he saw the face looking back at him from under the body. The eyes were packed with dirt, and the lips were parted by earth packed against the teeth. The flesh had taken on an ashen cast, the hair matted with clumps of blood-induced mud.

"Jesus," Stan sputtered. He pinched his eyes shut to try to chase the image away, but it remained, and he was forced to open his eyes and stare down the back of the cop's legs, at his soiled underwear.

Jim backed up the dirt ramp, looking over his shoulder every couple of steps, whether to watch his footing or make sure no one was coming, Stan wasn't sure, but he was terrified to even blink and potentially miss a car turning into the development or a jogger cutting through the cattails. Angling to the right, they passed the front of the adjacent foundation and continued walking until they were beside the one after that.

Jim stopped, letting go of the arms, and the body fell to the ground. The head bounced from the packed dirt. The forearms still stood erect, as they'd either broken or become dislocated at the elbows.

Stan followed suit and dropped the legs.

"Roll him in," Jim said. Stan watched him walk all the way back to where they had started before reappearing with the shovel.

Dropping to his knees in the dirt, Stan shoved both hands under the cop's lower back and growled with the exertion. The body toppled over the edge, all flapping arms and flailing legs, before doing a belly-flop on the leveled dirt below. A rush of wind escaped from it like a belch.

Stan knew why Jim had chosen this particular lot. The footers had already been poured and dried, and the iron framework for forming the walls and floor was on the trailer past the edge of the hole. The subcontractors would be pouring the concrete to finish the cement structure of the basement in the morning. And once the cement was laid and dried, it would take nothing shy of an act of God to lift the house out of the ground.

"You dig," Jim said, thrusting the shovel into Stan's chest.

It caught Stan completely off-guard. Never in the years he'd known his foreman had Jim ever so much as asked for anything, let alone made a demand. He'd always been agreeable to the hours of overtime and the extra work Stan would pile upon him at the last minute to rush a closing or maintain a deadline. Jim had never once raised his voice at Stan or contradicted him in any way.

"Okay," Stan said, wrapping both hands around the shovel and waiting for Jim to relinquish his grip before bringing it away from where it pressed against his sternum. He tried to read the expression on Jim's face, the thoughts behind his eyes, but the man was as stoic and unaffected as always.

Walking around to the end of the hole, Stan started down the slope, into the bottom of the pit, while Jim watched him from above, arms crossed over his barrel chest. Raindrops pattered the marsh while the wind rustled the leaves in the trees.

A flash of blue light strobed the sky, followed in due course by a rumbling sound.

Stan pointed the top of the shovel into the packed dirt in the middle of what would soon become the basement floor and braced his right foot on the upper lip beside the wooden shaft.

He stole his left hand away and slapped the side of his neck, swatting at a pair of mosquitoes. They hummed as they taunted him from just out of his reach.

Driving his foot down, Stan hauled out the first bite of the flattened dirt.

III

Stan swiped the back of his dirty hand across his brow and flung the rivers of sweat onto the ground. He felt as though he'd been used as a pincushion for all the resistance his shirt had provided against the onslaught of mosquitoes. Even though he swatted furiously at the cloud humming around him and slapped them as soon as he felt the stingers break the skin, his flesh crawled as though covered with millions of tiny feet.

The raindrops had grown larger, but fortunately the clouds had yet to release the full wrath of the storm. They snapped on the ground around him like bacon grease.

He stood knee-deep in the hole, his slacks coated with mud, a pile of excavated dirt beside him. The muscles in his arms and shoulders burned, and his lower back felt like a bent hinge preparing to snap, but he continued digging as fast as he could, knowing that the sooner they had the body under the ground, the sooner he could go back to his life and never have to think about this again.

Jim still supervised his efforts from above, watching him through eyes that looked almost predatory.

"You could…" Stan panted. He cleared his throat. "You could always help."

"I could," Jim said, but stayed right where he was.

"I'm just...starting to get really tired. Do you want to spell me...for just a minute?"

Jim didn't answer. Instead, he waited for Stan to drive the shovel into the ground and look up at him. Stan could have passed for one of those illegal aliens down there with stains in his pits and dirt sticking to his sweat like some kind of mud man. Under other circumstances, Jim would have laughed at the man down there in his expensive clothes, all dingy like a kid playing in the sandbox after Sunday school, but this was serious business, as business should always be treated.

"That's probably deep enough," he called down to Stan, who plopped down on the edge of the rectangular hole he'd created.

"Don't we want it to be six feet deep?"

"You worried about him rising from the dead?"

"No, I just—"

"It's deep enough," Jim said in a firm voice that quelled any sort of argument before it could even start.

"I guess they'll be pouring the foundation over it in the morning..." Stan muttered as if trying to convince himself.

"All that's left is to bury the body then," Jim said. He reached behind his back and removed the object he'd tucked into his pants between the flannel and the undershirt.

"Fine," Stan spat, tiring of this power struggle. He'd keep Jim on for a while, maybe six months or so, and then he'd find a way to pawn him off on one of his contractor friends. Jim was an amazing foreman. Anyone would want him. But Stan positively hated the thought of ever seeing the man again. He looked like he was enjoying himself up there, sniggering down at Stan. "I imagine I'll be doing that as well."

"You catch on fast," Jim said, palming the object behind his back.

All Stan wanted was to get out of there. If he had to push a dozen bodies down into that hole, he'd do it in a heartbeat, if it would get him out of the grave that much quicker. He walked around to the other side, where the cop lay prone with his broken nose bent to the side and his broken teeth dotting the ground like corn kernels.

Stan's pants were already ruined. It didn't matter now if any more dirt got on them or even if he tore the knees out. He was going to burn them as soon as he got home, anyway.

With a groan, Stan rolled the body up over its left side and flopped it on its back. He averted his eyes from the face, as that was the last thing in the world he wanted to see at that moment. Sliding his arms beneath it again, he rolled it one more time and it fell into the makeshift grave.

"Aren't you at least going to help me fill—?" Stan started. He turned around just in time to be momentarily blinded by a flash of light. Then another. And another. "What the hell are you doing?"

Jim brought the camera down from his eye and stuffed it back up between the shirts and tucked them again into his jeans.

"Let me tell you how this is going to work," Jim

said, his lips fixed in a tight line, eyes sharply focused. Lightning flashed, illuminating the clouds above. "Tomorrow morning you're going to sign over the deed granting me the land reserved for the final two phases of construction. I, in turn, will buy said tract of land for a year's salary: forty thousand dollars."

"The land's worth fifty times that!"

"You're right. Forty-thousand dollars is a paltry sum. That's what I've been trying to live on while busting my hump for *you*. To make *you* enough money to throw away in that mansion up in the hills. Forty thousand dollars. At least I had enough left over after the payments on my first and second mortgages, after the doubling of the price of the utilities, after getting reimbursed ten cents a mile when gas is four dollars a gallon…to buy myself a camera."

Tears drew lines through the dirt on Stan's cheeks. It felt as though his heart had stopped. The world around him slowed to a crawl. He was sure his stomach acids were already eating their way to freedom through his gut.

He dismissed the thought of rushing after Jim and trying to take the camera from him as soon as it entered his mind. He would have to run up the slope at the far end of the hole and then another twenty feet to reach where Jim was standing now. By the time he was even halfway there, Jim would be to his truck. And even if he somehow managed to catch the larger man, he wouldn't stand a chance in a skirmish without a weapon.

"What are you going to do with the pictures?" he finally asked.

"So long as you sell me the land for my price, these pictures will never leave my hands."

Stan nodded. His chin fell to his chest, and his shoulders slumped forward.

"And if you don't, you'll see them on the news."

"You can't go to the cops," Stan said, his voice faltering. "You're a part of this too."

"Who do you think they'll believe when they find his patrol car in your garage? Whose prints are on that shovel, huh?" Thunder crashed overhead as lightning pounded the ground somewhere on the western side of the lake. "They'll even find his clothes in your house."

Stan blubbered something incoherent as the sky opened the floodgates.

"Look at you!" Jim yelled. Lightning reflected from the rivulets of water draining down his face from his matted hair. "You're pathetic, you know that? Down there crying—"

A rush of warmth spattered Stan, who looked up to see Jim teetering above him on the edge of the pit, against the backdrop of a bolt of lightning, which whipped from side to side. Jim's eyes snapped open as wide as physically possible, and he vomited a geyser of blood. A jagged length of metal protruded from his upper abdomen. His body buckled back and forth before he fell to his knees, while the figure behind him tried to wrench its weapon back out. Jim's head lolled forward, and his body followed suit. He fell away from the lance with a slurping sound and plummeted down to the ground in the foundation.

Stan was already trying to run through the mud

in the opposite direction, slipping in his efforts to gain traction, falling repeatedly onto his stomach. The swarm of mosquitoes finally abandoned him and descended upon the heap of bleeding flesh. He looked up to where Jim had been only a moment prior, but there was no one else there.

"Help me!" he screamed, finally gaining some traction and lunging toward the opposite wall. He jumped and grabbed hold of the lip, but his fingers just carved through the mud like butter, dropping him to his knees.

He whirled around, but there was no one up on the edge of the cut. No one standing below it, where Jim's body was crumpled next to the cop's grave, a cloud of mosquitoes humming angrily around them. No one sprinting down the slope, into the foundation, which itself was beginning to feel more and more like one big grave.

"Help!" he screamed again. He floundered until he found his feet and leapt one more time for the lip, but he only ended up grabbing two handfuls of mud before slopping back down into the hole.

Stan slipped repeatedly before he finally gained his feet and ran as fast as he could toward the slanted exit. He was a third of the way up the slope when lightning pounded the stagnant water somewhere off in the marsh, lighting the entire area. A black shape stood directly in front of him, as though it had materialized from the very air itself. Living tatters of ebon fabric twisted from the form, like solar flares from the sun. He caught a flash of reflected lightning from eyes set deeply into the shadows beneath the cowl, from the wet blood still clinging to the arch of a rusted scythe, the handle a long, knotted willow trunk.

Stan screamed and threw himself in reverse. His legs slipped out from beneath him and he slid through the mud toward whatever that thing was. He managed to flip over onto his stomach and crawled back down into the hole before the lightning snapped off like a shattered overhead bulb.

A clap of thunder shook the ground.

Unable to push himself to his feet, Stan scrabbled toward the slowly-filling grave, seized the shovel, and spun to face the figure.

There was no one there.

He scanned the top of the walls around him, but he couldn't see anyone. Whoever was up there could easily have walked half a dozen paces back from the lip, and he wouldn't have been able to see them.

"Leave me alone!" Stan shouted into the rising wind.

Staking the spade into the soft ground, he pulled himself to his feet and tugged the shovel back out of the muck. Raising the metal scoop over his shoulder, he held it like a baseball bat, the muscles in his arms tensed in anticipation of swinging at the first sign of movement.

All he could hear was the patter of rain.

His heart raced, his breaths coming increasingly faster. The falling rain marred his vision like static.

"Where are you?" he yelled, though only the wind howled in response.

With a crackle of electricity, lightning ripped a seam in the sky.

Stan swung at a shadow that emerged from the furthest reaches of his peripheral vision. The shovel hammered something that felt as solid as a wall, emitting a loud clang. Jerking the shovel back again, he adjusted his grip, turned the blade of the scoop sideways, and prepared to swing with all his might.

A hand shot out from the wavering black form and grabbed a handful of Stan's shirt. He looked down and saw a fist so emaciated that it appeared skeletal, as though the skin had turned to parchment and dried right onto the bones. The phalanges and joints were so well-defined it looked more like a claw.

It pulled him closer, and in that fleeting second, no longer than the span of a single ventricular contraction, the thing's face was illuminated by the lightning. The eyes were the only part of it that appeared to be alive. They reflected wickedly, like polished marble set into deep sockets. All of the features were stretched taut, the nose like a canvas tent with twin teardrop slits up the front; the lips dried and peeled away from bared, brown teeth; the skin of the cheeks pulled so hard between the cheekbones and jaw-line that sections had snapped and torn away to expose the molars from the sides. Thin black veins forked through what remained of the dried epidermis.

There was a flash of silver and a sudden stinging sensation in his neck.

Next thing he knew he was looking up into the belly of the storm, electricity snapping from one cloud to the next. He took in a deep breath that sounded like a scream, but it felt as though someone had knocked the wind out of him. It wasn't until his head hit the ground and he saw his body fall to its knees in front of him, a whistling sound coming from the severed neck, that he understood what had happened. His head rolled until it settled with his right eye pressed into the mud, and he watched through his left in detached horror as his body crumpled forward into the mud.

The thing strode toward him, skeletal feet carving through the mud like talons beneath the bottom of the cloak. It reached down, rolled his head until he looked straight up into that face again, and drove its thumb through his right eye and its middle finger through his left. He felt their sharp tips touch somewhere behind in his sinuses.

The lightning died, and Stan knew a darkness like no other.

CHAPTER 14
SPECTRAL CROSSINGS

I

The portable x-ray machine was no longer of any use to them. Without a charge, it was little more than an enormous box of useless metal. Recharging was out of the question. The unit required four hundred and forty volts, and the standard household outlet delivered only half of that. And there was certainly no way that Steve could even think about taking it back to the hospital and waiting a couple hours for it to recharge, or stealing one of the other models. Besides, add grand theft to abandoning his shift, and the possibility of retaining his job was essentially nil. By this point, he didn't care though. He was so close to finally figuring out what had happened to his brother all those years ago, to finally being able to sleep through the night without waking to the image of that man in black hauling Brian off through the cattails.

Nothing else mattered now.

He'd told the others that he had to go home for a couple hours to get some sleep. Their plan was to wait until the afternoon storm and see if they could actually get some pictures of whomever the man in black was to turn over to the police, but that was far too passive for Steve. Instead of leaving the development, he'd driven as far back into the foothills as the roads went and waited. He'd dozed off pretty much immediately but had attuned his body to the world around him. At the first distant grumble of thunder, his eyes had snapped open, and he'd driven as close as he could without being out in the open, parking on the side of the road behind a stand of willows that obscured the car from the lake.

Waiting for the thunderstorm to roll in, watching the black clouds swelling like an atomic blast over the Rocky Mountains, Steve drew comfort from the cold steel clenched in his right fist, the feel of the barrel against his left thigh. The revolver had been a gift from his father once upon a time, a lingering remnant of the childhood stolen from him, which he intended to reclaim with that old 22-caliber pistol. It wasn't the kind of weapon that could drill a hole through a man or blow out the back of his skull, but a bullet to the heart or brain would be more than sufficient to kill. And unless he'd lost all of his skill over the last dozen years of no practice, he was confident he could hit one of those two spots. In fact, more than anything, he wanted to be looking into the man's terror-stricken eyes as he placed the barrel right between them and pulled the trigger. He wanted to smell the man's evacuated bowels, the copper tinge of his spilled blood. He wanted to feel the blood on his hands as it cooled. He wanted that man to look into his face as he died and remember the child whose life he had stolen so many years ago in this very swamp. And most of all, he wanted to avenge his brother.

Steve wasn't completely sold on this "String Theory," but the proof was sitting on the passenger seat next to him. An upper arm bone, a humerus. As a radiographer, if there was one thing he knew, it was bones, and this one was human. There was no mistaking it, as it was nearly the same length as his own, though thinner, the cortex denser. A teenager's bone.

The first flash of lightning crackled over the purple mountains.

He let out a long sigh, willing his pounding heart to slow. It felt like he was going to vomit. Slowly, he opened the door, welcoming the fresh air and the smell of ozone preceding the rending of the sky. His hand was trembling so badly that he could hardly force the barrel of the gun beneath his waistband, though he couldn't bring himself to release the grip. He needed to feel it in his hand, the reassurance of its weight and the coldness of its willingness to claim life without reservation.

Closing the car door, he didn't even bother to lock it. All of his effort was being used to focus his thoughts on the task at hand, keeping the fear and the nerves at bay. He could only imagine how he must look: covered in crumbling mud, the knees of his pants torn out to reveal a bloody crust, his hair a tangled nest of windblown knots. The creases in his knuckles were brown with dirt to match the packed crescents beneath his fingernails, as was the rest of his face, minus the trails the tears had eroded through them.

Lightning flared on the horizon behind him, stretching his shadow across the dirt road ahead and whipping it from side to side.

It felt as though his heart was beating so hard and fast it would break right through his ribcage. His right index finger toyed with the safety on the gun before slipping back beneath the trigger guard and tensing against the trigger.

II

Steve knew where he needed to go for things to come full circle. He needed to go back to the place where the man had stolen his brother from him, back to the very spot where he had last seen Brian. He could have found it in his sleep, as it haunted his every dream, but daylight proved more challenging. So much had changed since he'd last been there. So much. The gravel road leading to the dairy was now paved, the ruts now smooth asphalt. The dairy itself still stood, though only as a weathered and crumbling monument to its former glory. Where once hundreds of cattle had milled in shamrock-green pastures, there were now only twenty-some standing in knee-high weeds, now more feral than domesticated.

He stopped every fifty yards, trying to gauge his location, as nothing looked familiar. The first of the large raindrops tapped on his shoulders and head like skeletal fingertips. Where once seemingly eternal fields of cattails had stretched all the way back to the lake, there were now large copses of willows standing from the mire. Alkali chalk lined the edges of the water, the pungent residue of a time when the cattle hadn't been restrained by fences and slogged freely through the swamp. He remembered the red-tipped cottonwood saplings that had only been peeking up from the mud so long ago. Now they blocked the view of the lake from where he walked along the shoulder of the raised road, and lined the pasture beside him.

Some things never changed, though. The quacking of the mallards from somewhere out of sight. The splashing of whatever animals scampered through the reeds unseen. The patter of the rain on the marsh and the ozone that smelled like it had been freshly ripped from the sky. He imagined two boys in a different time, crashing through the cattails with their fly rods and creels, not even dreaming of the fortune they would find on the lake that day, or the fact that only one of them would be making the return trip.

His finger tightened on the trigger, and he had to completely remove it before he wound up shooting himself in the leg.

He was shaking, though he tried to rationalize it as shivering from the cold rain that now came down in a heavy drizzle. A blue strobe of lightning crackled off to his right.

"One one-thousand," he whispered. "Two one-thousand. Three—"

The crash of thunder cut him off and the rain began to fall harder.

There was the trickling sound of running water ahead, barely audible over the clapping of raindrops on the mire. He looked straight ahead and tried to estimate the distance to the dairy, imagining what the lights might look like after dark.

Steve knew he had to be close.

Another dozen paces and he could see where the stream cut through the pasture to the right and met with the side of the road. He looked to his left, and his heart skipped a beat.

Something sharp poked his neck, and he swatted it.

The rim of the corrugated metal tube poked out of the steep shoulder. The wide stretch of standing water in front of it was now ringed with tall willows, the long green leaves twinkling like stars as the rising wind bowed the branches from side to side. Cattails grew all around them, only starting to grow their fluffy brown tails. The puddle wasn't nearly as large as he remembered it, or the cattails as tall. The cottonwoods looming over the road from the other side hadn't even sprouted yet to cast their thick shadows across the road and onto the swamp.

He didn't realize until the first sob passed his lips that he was crying.

"Where are you?" he shouted, looking back over his shoulder at the lightning that flashed from the bellies of the clouds. Holding the pistol tightly in his right hand, he skidded down the gravel hillside and stopped right at the edge of the water, counting softly the whole while. "One one-thousand. Two one-thou—"

Thunder clapped in the electric sky and the earth quivered beneath him. He waved away a small cloud of swarming mosquitoes.

"Show yourself! You owe me that much!"

He prepared to step down into the cold water, but he remembered how it had felt with his brother's blood diluting into it.

"God damn you! Come out where I can see—"

A flash of lightning seared the darkening sky, and there, behind the swaying willow limbs and deep in the shadows of the reeds, he saw the bolt reflect from a pair of glassy eyes.

He pointed the pistol at those eyes and pulled the trigger. The foliage tore back in the bullet's passage, the report echoing louder than the thunder that chased the lightning into oblivion.

He ran forward, sloshing through the shin-deep water until he reached the wall of cattails, their long green leaves swishing from side to side as they had that night, after Brian had been hauled through them. Shoving the reeds out of his way, he exposed only more swamp water, not the bleeding body he had hoped to find. In fact, there was no blood at all, only the wispy seeds from inside the tails, which fluttered to the water like snowflakes.

"Where'd you go?" he screamed, turning in a circle. "Show your face, you coward!"

Had he really seen the lightning reflecting from a pair of eyes, or had it only been the stagnant water? It had certainly looked like a pair of eyes, but he knew that was what he *wanted* to see.

"Where are you?"

Lightning tore through the sky, and it was standing right in front of him, a black shape wavering on the edge of reality. Its cloak appeared fluid, as though reaching out with tentacles of tar, those eyes like liquid encapsulated in a thin film of gelatin the color of the night sky, the forks of electricity slashing diagonals across the sockets.

It felt like a garden spade ripped through his shirt and lacerated the skin of his abdomen as he raised the gun and jammed it against the creature's chest. He pulled the trigger as fingernails like fishhooks latched under his skin and tried to tear their way free.

Steve heard himself screaming, and something like a hoarse shriek came from the shrouded darkness only inches from his face. He tasted warm breath that reeked of sepsis on his lips. There was a tug under his flesh, and he was pulled off of his feet.

The lightning faded to memory, washed away by the growl of thunder overhead.

Blood diffused in the choppy water as the ripples widened and expanded outward toward the banks.

Parabolic cups of rain pocked the surface of the stilling water.

Somewhere behind the thunderheads, the sun dipped behind the Rockies, leaving only the hint of the rising moon to watch over the empty swamp.

III

"Did you hear that?" Teri gasped. She glanced out the kitchen window toward the origin of the sound.

"Hear what?" Kevin asked, setting his cup of coffee back onto the saucer.

"It sounded like a gunshot."

"Probably just thunder."

"No," she said, rising from the kitchen table and walking to the window. She drew back the sash and looked through the water-spotted glass. The rain was really starting to come down now. Her unseeded back yard was a sloppy stretch of mud and growing puddles. "I know what thunder sounds like, this was—"

Lightning stabbed the ground, illuminating the entire lake behind her house. She took an unconscious step backwards.

The intense smell of ozone seeped through the seal of the window.

"Not…thunder…"

The floor vibrated and the windowpanes rattled as a grumble of thunder started from the west and passed over them to the east.

"Was that what you heard?" he asked.

"No," she said, drawing the window open a couple of inches. A mosquito landed on the screen, followed by several others. Beneath the patter of rain, she could hear the crackle of her bug zapper. "It sounded more like—"

A loud *bang* silenced her.

Its echo drifted off across the plains.

"That," Teri finished. She leaned closer to the window to try to see through the amoeboid globules of rain and the swarming insects.

Kevin stood and nearly knocked the chair to the floor. The color drained from his face. He knew the sound of gunfire. Knew it all too well. It was the sound that dissipated with the residue of his nightmares upon waking, the first sound to welcome him into unconsciousness' embrace. It was the abrupt sound of his brother's death and the end of the world as he had known it.

Teri turned to ask him if he'd heard it that time, but the look on his face was unmistakable. He had definitely heard it.

"You don't think that was…?" she asked.

"Steve?"

"Yeah."

"We haven't seen a cop car since the forensics crew left this morning."

"I thought he said he was going home to get some rest before the storm hit."

"In case you haven't noticed, the storm's already here."

"We have to help him," she said, dashing toward the stairs that led down into the family room.

Kevin caught her by the arm.

"Where do you think you're going?"

"We can't just leave him out there all alone."

"What we need to do is call the police."

"Fine," she said, jerking her arm out of his grasp. "You call the police. At least one of us needs to make sure that he isn't lying in the swamp bleeding to death."

"And how much help could you possibly be if you were dying there beside him?"

She paused at the top of the stairs and looked back at him.

"I watched that girl get ripped apart right in front of me last night. I'll never forget the look of terror in her eyes." Her voice dropped to a whisper. "She never had a chance. For all we know, Steve's already gone."

"We need to wait for the police." Part of him hated himself for sounding so scared. What if he'd heard his brother shuck the shell into the chamber of the shotgun in the middle of the night? Would he have cowered in bed, waiting for someone else to check on him?

"Bo," she called. There was the clatter of nails against the outside of the sliding glass door, which she drew open to the sound of jangling dog tags.

"Wait," he said. He closed his eyes and tried to steady his trembling hands. "Wait for me."

Kevin pulled his cell phone from his pocket and scrolled through the speed dial menu until he found Darren's name. With a click of the "send" button, he brought the dialing phone to his ear as he walked down the stairs. His legs were shaking so badly that he momentarily feared he might fall.

Teri was waiting for him on the back porch, beneath the overhang, holding the leash while the big lab sat on the concrete pad, watching the swirling cloud of mosquitoes popping like little blue firecrackers on the bug zapper.

"Hi. I'm not able to get to the phone right now. If this is an emergency, please try my cell phone—" Kevin silenced his friend's voice with a click and then dialed Darren's cell.

"Give me just a minute," he said, holding up a finger.

Teri turned toward the lake.

The only sound was the rain drumming in the reeds.

"This is Officer Darren Drury with the—"

He hung up again.

This time he dialed 911.

"Emergency services," a harried voice answered. "What's the nature of your emergency?"

"There have been shots fired at Kettner Lake," he said, glancing up at Teri, who had already started across the muddy yard.

IV

Steve fell to his knees in the small creek. He dropped the gun and grabbed for his stomach. The hot barrel sizzled when it hit the water.

It felt as though his abdomen had been opened and his guts ripped right out. He could feel the warmth of the blood on his hands.

"Jesus," he gasped, rolling his quivering hands palm up so that he could see them. They were dripping with blood, but not nearly as much as he'd expected. Part of him had imagined that as soon as he moved his hands, a loop of intestines would drop out and a rush of blood would spatter the stream, but it must have felt far worse than it actually was.

He braved a peek at his stomach. There were four long gashes that would definitely require stitches, but they appeared mostly superficial. There was one spot toward the middle of each where the skin curled back to the point that he thought he could see the striations of the muscles beneath, but he forced himself not to think about it.

"I know...you're still there," he whispered.

Pulling his shirt over his head, he wrapped it around his midsection and tied it as tightly as he could. He screamed when the fabric bit down on his wounds.

Biting his lip through the pain, he staggered to his feet in the knee-deep, ice-cold water, and swayed as he fought the dizziness from the blood loss.

"Show yourself."

He turned in a slow circle, peeling apart every shadow, studying every swaying branch and minute sound.

There had been a moment when he'd felt whatever that thing was wrench its claws out of his gut, but his eyes had been pinched shut in agony, and he hadn't seen where it had gone. Had it simply vanished like it had before?

The gun was somewhere down in the muck beneath the cloud of the turned bed, but even if he were able to sift through the mire and find it, the chances of it functioning were minimal. The prospect of blowing his whole arm off while trying to shoot that thing was unappealing. He should turn back, go get help, but he'd come so far now…so far…

Sloshing forward, he crashed through the wall of reeds.

He felt increasingly disoriented. It took all of his concentration to put one foot in front of the other while fighting his way through the cattails.

"Come on. Where'd you go?"

He had to stop to catch his breath and doubled over to cradle his abdomen. The pain was becoming more than he could bear. There was no choice but to simply let the humming cloud of mosquitoes descend upon him, as he didn't have the energy to waste swatting them.

There was a crashing sound ahead and to his left.

Somehow his body found the strength to propel him forward once again.

He could only spare one hand to push aside the weeds, as he needed the other to hold the stinging wounds closed.

The most horrific scent overwhelmed him. It began as the normal foul smell of swamp, rotten egg gas burbling up through decomposition, but became something more…corporeal. It had a texture to it, almost like an oily film that he could feel dripping into his pores, forming a layer of grunge inside his nose and mouth. After a moment, he had to pull his bloody hand from his stomach to cover his nose and mouth so he wouldn't become violently sick. The awful aroma had mutated into something positively gut-wrenching, a vile mixture of long-since-expired meat and an indescribable biological taint.

He stumbled out onto a path through the cattails, trampled reeds beneath standing water and mud. It led off to the left into a bank of violently shaking willows that swallowed the path.

Lightning flared above, staining the entire world around him a pale shade of blue.

He stopped and looked at the sky in time to see the neon fork of electricity snap back up into the clouds, their black bellies flashing an angry red. He'd never seen anything like it. All of the hairs on his body stood fully erect, as though a charge were being passed through him. Even his skin tingled.

His first thought was that he was about to be electrocuted, that the lightning had struck the water and the lethal charge was racing toward him through the swamp, and that he was only feeling the leading edge of it, but when he climbed up out of the water onto a trampled mess of fallen cattails, he could still feel the current inside of him. He looked down at his feet to make sure that they weren't still in contact with the water—

The ground was covered with bones in various states of disarray and decomposition. Some were so small they looked almost like gravel, but rocks didn't splinter like these did, nor were they lined with fine grooves. Away from the beaten path, the bones were much larger. And they were everywhere. What he had assumed to be tangles of weeds and fallen branches trying to trip him as he ran had been bones. The whole swamp was full of them.

Steve raised his eyes to the wall of shrubs ahead.

Behind those branches was the source of the smell, the small enclave where they had experimented with the portable x-ray machine earlier. This was where that creature brought its victims, their remains scattered around him. This was where it brought them to die.

He suddenly wished he'd fished through the silt to find his pistol. Even had it jammed and exploded in his face, that would have been a pleasant death compared to what surely transpired beyond the willows ahead.

Standing there, with the gusting wind pelting him with rain from a dozen different angles at once, he thought about Brian. Had his brother ended up on the other side of those trees? He remembered the screaming image, the sheer agony on Brian's face as it faded from the radiograph, the skull he had x-rayed in the morgue. The metal bolted to its face. The cracks in the cranium from blunt trauma. The missing teeth and shattered jaw.

He had to know.

Unadulterated rage welled inside him, eclipsing the fear.

Barely able to see through the raindrops and tears, he sobbed and sprinted toward what would surely be his death.

V

"Do you see anything?" Teri shouted. She didn't know exactly where Kevin was, and couldn't see him over the cattails surrounding the thin path. Bo raced from one side to the other, crashing through the dead husks and jerking on her arm as he tested the tether.

"No," he called back from somewhere to her left, his voice distant and strained.

Lightning flashed, and the air around her crackled with electricity. The night sky reminded her of television static with all of the mosquitoes buzzing overhead.

Movement directly ahead down the path caught her eye.

"Steve!" She sprinted toward him, but as soon as the strobe faded, there was no one at all ahead of her on the path. "Steve!"

She ran to where she had seen him and stopped. The reeds to either side jostled on the wind. She hadn't seen him duck off the path to either side.

"Steve?" she called, taking another step. The path terminated ahead of her, against a wall of trees. Had there been anyone there, she would have easily been able to see them.

Thunder shook the earth.

She was sure she had seen him though. In that brief moment. There was no mistaking it. His back had been to her. He had been hunched over as though carrying something heavy against his belly. The lightning had outlined his hair and the side of his face. She'd even seen him take a hobbling step forward.

Where could he possibly have gone?

"Steve?" she whispered.

The rising wind blew a chill up her spine, and she had to wrap her arms around her chest for warmth. Hackles rose along her triceps. It was the sensation her mother had described as "someone walking over your grave," but it felt more like someone had walked right through her.

"Steve?"

Bo whined and tugged on the leash, spurring her to motion. A throng of barking erupted from him as he fought against the constraints of the leash, struggling to move faster than she would allow.

"Bo, heel."

He just continued barking, the hairs rising along his back. Finally, he wrenched the loop of the leash out of her hand, darted ahead, and stopped right before he reached the apparent end of the path. He lowered his head, and his back and fell as he ate something off of the ground.

"No!" she shouted, but he acted as though he hadn't heard.

"...all right?" Kevin's voice drifted toward her on the breeze.

She glanced back over her shoulder, hoping he was somewhere close enough to be seen, but the wind blew the reeds sideways across the path behind her, obscuring her vision of anything. Turning, she ran down the path toward Bo.

"Drop it," she commanded, jerking him by the collar.

He fought against her, and repeatedly shoved his muzzle into the mire until she was forced to pull him up off his front legs and to his rear haunches.

"Damn it, Bo. Would you just leave it alo—"

His muzzle was covered in blood nearly up to his eyes. At first it had thought it was some kind of oil, slick and shimmering under the fresh crack of lightning, but then she noticed the spatters on the trampled weeds.

When she looked up, Steve was there again, at the end of the path, standing with his back to her. His shoulders rose as he took in a deep breath and reached for the branches to pull them back.

The lightning vanished with the grumble of thunder, and then he was gone. The branches he had moved fell back into place as though blown from by a wind that didn't affect the rest of the tree.

"Kevin!" she shouted, letting go of Bo's collar. The dog went right back to the mess and began tearing out mouthfuls of swamp grass. "Kevin!"

She had seen Steve this time. Without a doubt. He had been there one moment and then gone the next, as though he had simply ceased to exist. And both times she had seen him during a lightning strike. There was a brief moment where the professional in her reveled in knowing that she had been right, that for whatever reason this place allowed for the right combination of electrical charges to tilt the spinning of the atoms to just the right degree as to permit a dimensional shift, but those feelings were quickly shoved aside by the overwhelming fear.

"Are you okay?" Kevin gasped, emerging from the reeds beside Teri.

She turned to look at him, her eyes wide, face pale.

She opened her mouth as if to say something, then quickly looked away. He followed her gaze to the rustling mass of willows. Somehow he had known that they would end up back here, where they had looked through the window to the other side and seen the remains of unparalleled horrors. He thought of the hand staked to the trunk of the tree and the bones dangling from the canopy.

"We should really just wait for the police," he said.

"I saw Steve go in there. Not on this plane, but on the other. He's in there with whatever did all of those horrible things."

"We can't—" he started, but Teri was already walking slowly ahead. He grabbed her hand, but she jerked it away.

When she reached the end of the path, she turned around and looked at him. With the rain pouring down her face, he couldn't tell if she was crying, but she looked like a little girl standing there, with her clumped hair hanging down over her face.

"You don't have to…" he said. Every instinct screamed for him to turn around, run back to his car, and drive home where everything was warm and safe, but deep down he knew that on the other side of that line of foliage was the answer to the questions that had haunted him for years. "Stay here. I'll go…."

Kevin closed his eyes as he spoke those final words, surprised to hear them actually come out of his mouth.

He reached past Teri, felt the wet leaves against the back of his hand as he pried them back, and exposed a maw of darkness from which a wave of coldness washed over him. There was a buzzing sound from deep within. Small insect bodies materialized from the shadows to tap against his face.

With his heart beating hard and fast, he ducked his head and inched forward through the willows.

A cold hand slipped into his. He looked back only long enough to see Teri's frightened face, swallowed the knot of fear, and plunged into the darkness.

VI

The sky came to life with dueling bolts of lightning.

Steve's head grew light and he fell to his knees. The impact with the ground caused a swell of blood to wash over his hand, which seemed to be losing the battle with his open gut. Groaning, he struggled back to his feet, and swayed momentarily before staggering forward.

"I know you're in there," he whispered as the shadows raced in to fill the void left by the lightning.

He stood before the willows and drew a great inhalation to try to steady his vision. He was stalling, and he knew it. All he wanted to do was lie down on the ground and close his eyes for a little while, but he'd be able to do that soon enough. Soon a lifetime of anguish would be resolved, and he could let go of the guilt and pain.

Soon.

The wind rose with a howl, and on it he thought he heard his name called from a distance.

He thrust out his right arm and parted the willows like a curtain, releasing the trapped aromas of death and decay, as though prying open the beak of a vulture. Branches clawed at him, trying to ward him off, but they merely slowed him down as he stepped through into the darkness, where the breeze couldn't follow him.

Everything was black. The humidity was so thick that it felt like liquid fingers tracing his skin, until a buzzing cloud descended upon him. High-pitched whining filled his ears as tiny bodies tapped at his earlobes and cheeks, though the majority crawled all over his hand and bleeding abdomen. Beneath that sound was something else, a clacking sound like chattering teeth.

"Where are you?" he whispered, limping forward, one arm moving side to side in front of him like a blind man's cane.

The smell was now a texture on his tongue, but it didn't matter with the reflux of blood filling his mouth.

There was a crackle of electricity, and slanted lines of blue light pierced the canopy like lasers. Bones dangled in front of him, some still covered with blue flesh, minus the black holes where bites had been stolen. A man he didn't recognize dangled by his heels from above, his feet staked with rusted rebar through the intertwined branches. Long segments of hollow bones had been stabbed into him from many different angles. Blood drained out of them like spigots into the waiting bull craniums below, which were full to overflowing. There was a skin of mosquitoes on the fluid, swirling around the draining lines of blood.

He heard the chattering sound from somewhere to his left and turned in time to see the pale light reflect from twin slits of eyes.

Thunder boomed as the light again abandoned them in the darkness.

Steve reached for the body dangling in front of him, and felt along the man's flank until he found a pulpy wound and the length of sharpened bone sticking out from it like a porcupine's quill. He gripped it and yanked it out with a crack and a slurping sound. The remainder of the blood passing through it dripped onto the crackling collection of bones beneath his feet.

He listened for the chattering, attuning his hearing to the sound over the crunch of his tread and the hum of the mosquitoes.

"I got you, didn't I?" he said.

There was only a hiss in response.

"Do you remember me? Hmm?"

He eased forward, adjusting his grip on the sharpened bone. There was a scrabbling sound in the darkness, of something trying desperately to get away.

"You killed my brother!" he screamed. "Right in front of me!"

Another hiss bled into the chattering sound.

Steve swung the bone in front of him, the hollow medullary cavity making it whistle.

Lightning struck again, and thin beams crisscrossed the darkness.

"Steve?" someone said from behind him, but he didn't turn.

Another man's corpse had been stretched between two trunks ahead, his hands staked to the wood, his shoulders disjointed so that he hung limply. His chest had been cracked open, the shattered ribs widened like a toothy mouth around the hollow cavity where his lungs and heart had once been. The skin had been peeled away, stretched to reach the trees, and pinned in place with bent nails. It reminded him of the squirrels he had seen so many years ago, which had been in his nightmares ever since. Where the head should have been was nothing but a collection of ragged tendons and tattered vessels.

He looked back to the thing crouched on the ground, which stared up at him with lightning reflected in wide, lidless eyes.

Squeezing the bone in both hands, he raised it high over his head and aligned the sharpened tip with the crown of the creature's head.

"This is for Brian," he said, and drove the stake down with a crack of breaking bone.

"Steve!" a voice shouted from directly behind him. He felt a tug on the back of his shirt.

Thunder echoed like a gunshot, killing the light.

VII

The smell hit Kevin as soon as he stepped into the darkness. He'd never smelled anything so revolting in his entire life. It was how he imagined it might have smelled exhuming the bodies from the mass burials at Auschwitz.

"Dear God," he gasped, clapping his free hand over his mouth.

Teri retched behind him.

Bo whimpered from outside the natural enclosure, where he had planted his rear end in the muck and refused to take another step. Teri had tugged against him several times before simply dropping the leash.

"The police should be here any second," Kevin whispered, more for his own reassurance than hers.

The humming grew frenetic around him, and he had to release her hand to slap at the crawling sensation all over his body.

Kevin stretched his arms out and moved them slowly from side to side, so as not to stumble into anything, anyone.

Pinpoints of light fired down through the canopy from the lightning above, and his right hand smacked into something soft and forgiving. The man appeared right in front of him as though he drew form from the shadows. He had been strung up by his ankles and fluid drained out of tubes that could only have been bones, which stuck out of his body at awkward angles.

He saw movement to his left.

"Steve?"

A man stood with his back to him, doubled over slightly, but if it were Steve, he didn't respond. The man pulled a bloody hand from his abdomen and raised a long section of broken bone high over his head with both hands, like a knight preparing to drive his sword down through a fallen enemy's heart.

"This is for Brian," the figure said, and Kevin immediately knew he'd been right.

"Steve!" he shouted, grabbing him by the back of the shirt and pulling as Steve slammed down the bone with a sickening crack.

With a clap of thunder, the darkness raced in and abolished the light.

Kevin tried to maintain his balance as Steve toppled backwards into him, but they both ended up careening to the ground. His shoulder clipped a tree trunk, and a spire of pain shot down his arm. Lights blossomed in his vision as his head hit the ground.

"No!" Steve screamed, struggling to crawl off of Kevin. "I had him!"

Kevin rolled over and crawled ahead until he felt leaves on his face. He pushed through and continued crawling until his hands sunk into mud and rain slapped his head. Teri followed and stood over him, both hands covering her mouth and nose.

"Oh God. Are you okay?" she asked, dropping to her knees. She lifted his chin with both hands and looked into his eyes as he forced himself to rise to his feet.

He nodded, but couldn't seem to find his voice.

"What are you doing?" Steve shouted, bursting out

through the willows. He staggered right up to Kevin and shoved him. "I had it, damn it! It was right there, and I had it!"

Kevin stumbled backwards, nearly tumbling into the cattails.

"I was trying to save you."

"He was right there—"

"We heard gunfire."

"—and I had him dead to rights!"

"I thought…"

"You thought? You thought what? Jesus Christ, I—"

Lightning filled the sky as if the world had caught fire.

Steve turned as the creature appeared behind him. Claws pierced his left flank and probed within him. He grabbed the bone standing out of the thing's black head, and, screaming, gripped it as tightly as he could, driving it downward. The claws tore straight down his side, and finally ripped out of the skin in the middle of his thigh. It hissed as he slammed its head to the ground. His left arm fell to his side, but it was useless against the deluge of blood that poured out through his tattered clothes. He struggled to breathe through the pain. Holding the shaft of the bone in his right hand, he shoved it down until it made a cracking sound. The bone emerged from the base of the creature's cranium and lanced through the soft tissue inside the arch of the mandible. There was a solid *thuck* as the sharpened tip embedded in the mud.

Thunder grumbled, and the world again welcomed the embrace of darkness.

Steve dropped to his knees beside it, no longer able to stand.

Chattering, the thing tried to raise its head. Its fingers combed through the mud, clawing out clods of dirt and weed roots.

Steve crawled in front of it, so he could look it directly in the eyes. He imagined that he could see the fear and recognition in the creature's eyes, swirling in the liquid depths of those gelatinous orbs. Collapsing to his stomach, the world teetering to either side as though he were balanced on a fulcrum, Steve stared at that awful face through eyes no longer even able to bat away the raindrops that rolled down his forehead and through his eyebrows. The features were remarkably human, though aged well beyond even the ravages of time. The skin was dry and stretched so tightly over the facial bones that it appeared skeletal. Its cheekbones protruded through vertical seams that had been ripped through the parchment flesh to expose the chattering yellow teeth in the bloody mouth. There was no longer cartilage in its nose, merely a triangular patch of skin and a pair of matching slits.

The wail of sirens drifted across the swamp, and the distant sky absorbed the blue and red glow of the swirling lights.

"Don't try to move," Teri said, crouching beside Steve. "Help's on the way."

Steve looked up at her from the corners of his eyes, and fought to remain conscious. The hint of a smile traced his lips.

Lightning filled the sky.

The creature's right hand rose from the mud and slashed him straight down the face. Those wicked claws split his upper eyelids and eyeballs before snagging the lower lids and hanging by them. The skin stretched to its limits before tearing down his cheeks.

Steve screamed.

Teri toppled to her rear end in the sludge, and tried to pull the thing's fingernails out of Steve's face, which now bled freely from the eyes.

"Hold still! Hold still!" Kevin sputtered. He crouched on the other side of Steve, and held out his trembling hands as he debated how best to remove the skeletal hand from where it had latched onto Steve's face.

Thunder roared and shook the ground.

The blue strobe of light lingered a moment longer, highlighting Steve's contorted face, and then faded.

Kevin and Teri knelt on the ground, staring blankly at each other. There was nothing on the ground between them but a wash of blood on the mud and reeds.

The sirens grew louder, and beneath them the sounds of tires splashing through puddles. The entire swamp turned blue and red, and the rain glowed with it as it fell to the earth.

Footsteps sloshed through the mire beyond the walls of reeds. There was shouting, but the words dissolved into the storm.

Lightning shredded the sky, and illuminated only the bare ground between them.

CHAPTER 15

THE SPACE BETWEEN
A BLINK AND A TEAR

I

Kevin sat in bed, the covers bunched around his waist. His laptop computer rested on his legs while some late night talk show or other played on the television across the room. There was a textbook of sorts on the bed beside him with dozens of torn pieces of paper marking pages where select passages were highlighted. *The Physics of the Mind* by Dr. Gustav Feiner, MD. He was trying to formulate the theory that seemed to be sitting right at the forefront of his mind. It was an intangible spectre of an idea, and he was struggling to find the words to express it.

Really, he was just trying to occupy himself in any way he possibly could to keep from going to sleep.

It had been three days now. The police had been through every inch of that swamp, searching for any trace of the five people who had disappeared in the span of twenty-four hours. A group of workers had found Darren's stripped body under a mound of dirt in the bottom of one of the holes in which they were preparing to pour a foundation. There would be a parade followed by a departmental burial the day after next. The papers speculated that one of the dirt roads out there in that development would be renamed in his honor, but it would seriously surprise Kevin if they even finished construction out there. Several houses already had "For Sale" signs staked in their lawns, and half a dozen contracts had been canceled.

The authorities were only now beginning to broaden their search for April Pettenger, whose mother suspected that her daughter must have run off with some boy or other to "teach her a lesson." The blood in the drainage pipe had been conclusively determined to have belonged to her, but without a body, there was no way of officially calling her deceased. When her mother finally opened her eyes to the situation, she would panic and hang herself the same year they posted pictures of her missing daughter on the bulletin boards at the front of every WalMart in the state.

The search for Stan Garnet had led to the discovery of Officer Darren Drury's police cruiser in his garage. Several partial fingerprints had been lifted from the interior of the squad car and linked to the construction magnate's foreman, Jim Savage. Those found on a shovel near where Darren had been unearthed belonged to Stan himself. It hadn't been a stretch to demonstrate that it was the same shovel that had been used to bury the deceased officer. The pieces of the puzzle had been relatively easy to assemble for the detectives after that. Darren had confronted either Stan or Jim about the bones they had found in Kettner Lake. Understanding the financial ramifications of such a discovery, Stan and Jim had killed Darren and tried to cover their tracks. All of Stan's money remained accounted for, but in the construction business, embezzling from himself wouldn't have been too terribly difficult. For all they knew, he was living it up on some island or other, sipping Mai Tais with natives in coconut bras.

Though the police would keep their eternal watch after the murder of one of their own, neither man would ever be seen again.

They had found Steve's car a couple miles away, where he had abandoned it, and a moving truck rented in his name. In the cargo bed had been a portable x-ray machine stolen from his former employer, who had begun his termination paperwork the afternoon of his disappearance. Interviews with the few casual acquaintances Steve kept turned up nothing of any formal use. All described him as a quiet guy who kept to himself, the kind who no one would be surprised to find out had simply up and left. His closet was full of clothes, and the food in his refrigerator was still within the expiration date. All of the bill payments were current. The only clue to his disappearance had been psychological evaluations that described him as depressed and possibly suicidal. The common assumption was that he had waded into the same lake in which his brother had drowned so many years prior, and shot himself. They had found his recently-fired gun and imagined that his body was somewhere in the marsh. The police had dredged the lake for his body, but even the divers hadn't found a thing.

That was no surprise, of course, as there had been several corpses through the years that had vanished in the marsh, and taken more than a decade and a half to resurface.

Kevin had tried to explain what had happened, but no one had listened. No one wanted to hear what even he thought sounded like the ravings of a lunatic. That was why he needed to distance himself from the situation, if only by degree, to allow himself the ability to approach the scenario from a clinical and detached perspective.

To rationalize it for himself, so that maybe he could understand and accept what had happened.

So that maybe he could sleep.

Sir Isaac Newton's Third Law of Motion states that for every action there is an equal and opposite reaction, which applies to the physical world of opposing forces. Feiner postulated that the mind was a closed system, and that within, the brain's electrical activity was obligated to obey the same laws of physics as the world without. And while he speculated about the neural and chemical interactions specifically, Kevin guessed that the same principles applied to the less tangible aspects of psychology. So for every release of a stimulant, there was a corresponding release of a depressant. For every thought there was an equally strong anti-thought. If a thought could be defined as a conscious mental process of logic, then an anti-thought could be described as an unconscious, indefinable stretch of the imagination. The opposite of a thought was a dream. So for every rational worry or obsession that plagued the waking mind, there was an equally intense, though irrational, nightmare waiting beyond the doors of sleep.

A man feeling guilty about sending his mother to a nursing home might dream about when he was grounded to his room as a child.

Someone who received too much change for a purchase and said nothing may dream about losing his wallet or having too little money to buy what he wanted.

Or a child who thought he should have been able to save his brother's life and blamed himself for having not, might dream of his brother dying over and over again.

Kevin nodded to himself and set the laptop beside the book. He could type it up in the morning. That was the kind of theory in which dozens of academic journals would be interested. The most difficult aspect of psychology is that there is never concrete proof, so one can only prove it to himself and hope his convictions come across in his presentation. He needed to change his conscious thoughts in order to rid himself of his nightmares.

Rubbing his eyes, he turned off the TV, which had been on for the endless days since he had walked away from the lake where his brother's girlfriend had died. He finally understood why Kyle had chosen to end his life as well. Perhaps exhaustion was twisting his thoughts and making pseudo-sense out of nonsense, but in the middle of the night, while wrestling with the symptoms of sleep deprivation, it made complete sense.

"It wasn't my fault," he whispered, reaching back to flip the switch on the light.

Darkness encroached from all sides, but it didn't feel as cold as it normally did.

"There was nothing I could have done."

He felt his irises rolling upward under his closed lids, the most wonderful sensation he could imagine.

"I was just…a little…kid…"

His whispers trailed into silence.

The last thought to cross his mind, straddling the line between consciousness and dreams, was that if Newton was right and there was an equal and opposite reaction for every action, what had they done by killing that creature?

Images flooded his sleeping mind. For the first time, they weren't preceded by the sound of gunfire and his mother's screams.

II

The skeletal domiciles lining the road to either side hadn't changed in the month since she'd been here. Giant rectangular holes in the ground now held several feet of murky brown water, which appeared more like abandoned swimming pools than the foundations they had once been dug to house. The others were arrested in various degrees of completion, from basements that would never see framework above them to houses missing only their shingles. "For Sale" signs lined the front yards. All of the "Under Contract" placards had been pulled down and replaced by graffiti. The realtors on the signs now all had spray-painted mustaches and blackened teeth. Tarps covered stacks of waterlogged lumber, and several earthmovers stood between the houses, preparing to rust their way into the dirt. Broken windows were haphazardly boarded up, the glass still littering the ground where by now there should have been lawn. Even most of the fully completed houses had "For Sale" signs in front of them as moving trucks came and went, ushering families out of the development and leaving only emptiness in their stead. Some still tried to continue with their lives as normal, while everything around them deteriorated. After all, walking away from a home and losing every cent of equity while still being burdened with the payments was a miserable financial prospect, but one that many of her former neighbors had been willing to bear.

Candles had burned to molten stumps and fused to the concrete in pools of their own wax on several street corners. They were surrounded by the dead husks of flowers where vigils had been held for April Pettenger. The poster board signs adorned by her picture were now warped beyond repair by the elements and crumpled against the upstart weeds amidst a scattering of dried petals. April's family was one of the few that remained, knowing that if they moved away, their daughter would never be able to find them when she returned, though from the state of her memorial, even they appeared to be losing hope.

Teri tried not to think about it, but not a minute had gone by that she hadn't. The memories were with her all the time and wherever she went. At first Kevin had tried to stay in contact with her, but every time she heard his voice, all she could think of was the look on Steve's face when that thing had carved through his eyes, and that perilous moment where his lower lids had stretched to their limits before finally ripping right down the center and—

She shuddered away the image, goosebumps rising up her shoulders.

This would be the last time she walked through this neighborhood. She was content to walk away and live in a loft downtown. Granted, the money tied up in the house had been her legacy from her parents, but she was sure they would have understood.

There was a part of her that was hoping for some sort of closure, though she didn't know what she was looking for, or if she would recognize it if she found it. All she knew was that she needed to come back one last time to end the saga in her own way. When she had left before, she had done so running. She needed to stare down her demons on her own terms, or she feared they would follow her wherever she went.

Perhaps she'd come back because she was no closer to understanding how the electrostatic discharge of the lightning had opened the rift between their world and the next. Her String Theory correlation was sound, at least theoretically, but she had yet to successfully recreate the conditions to provide conclusive proof.

None of that mattered now anyway.

She just needed to close this chapter of her life and try to forget everything she'd seen.

Bo trotted ahead of her, at the end of his leash. She could tell that even the dog didn't want to be back there. The entire area had a tainted feel to it, as though even the air had been scarred by the events of the month prior.

As she approached her car, which she had parked in front of what had once been her house, she heard the growl of thunder. She'd been too distracted to notice that the storm had slipped over the peaks unheralded.

Now, all she wanted was to get as far away from there as possible. She hadn't so much as looked out the window during a rainstorm since that night. The weather report had predicted a twenty percent chance of afternoon showers, but there hadn't been a cloud in the sky when she'd left her loft. That was one of the mysteries of Colorado weather. It could change in a heartbeat without the slightest warning.

"Come on, Bo," she said, breaking into a jog.

When she reached the car, she opened the back door and unclipped Bo's leash. His haunches tensed as he prepared to leap up onto the seat, but he paused and cocked his head, his floppy ears twitching. He looked at her, their eyes locking, and then sprinted away from the car and down the hill into the cattails.

"Get back here! Bo, come!"

She heard the crash of dry reeds and could barely make out the tops of the weeds swaying before his advance.

"Bo!" she screamed, running to the edge of the cattails and stopping abruptly.

Looking back over her shoulder, she marked the distance from the storm as the first droplet of rain tapped her cheek.

"Please, God…" she whispered, turning again to the wall of reeds that swished back and forth before her. Raising her arms in front of her face, she tried to follow Bo's path.

She had to hurry. She absolutely couldn't stand the idea of being out there in the swamp where she wouldn't be able to see anything but the thunderheads as they grew darker and eclipsed the sky.

"Bo! God damn it! Come!"

He began to bark from somewhere ahead, a furious throng that seemed to grow louder and more insistent with each passing second.

A mosquito hummed in her ear.

Tears raced down her cheeks, and her heartbeat accelerated.

The sound of barking grew closer and closer, overpowering even the crunching of dead weeds and the slapping of her feet on the thin layer of standing water.

"Bo?" She slowed when she saw his fur flirting in and out between the blowing stalks. He had his head lowered and his ears forward, his upper lip curled back from his bared canines as he barked uncontrollably.

She reached out with a shaking hand, pressed back the cattails to grant her passage, and stepped into a small circle of matted brush. Bo stood rigid, unflinching, just barking at the bowed weeds in front of him.

She breathed a jerky sigh of relief, walked up to his side, and placed her hand on his erect back fur, ruffling it to chase off a pair of mosquitoes.

"It's okay," she whispered. She leaned forward and clipped the leash back onto his collar. "We'll find you a park with some ducks by our new place, and I'll let you chase them to your heart's content. Maybe we'll even find some squirrels for you to—"

Her words died as lightning crackled over the foothills behind her.

Where a split-second prior there had been nothing, there was now a black heap. At first it looked like some sort of animal with hair like a bear, long locks flagging on the breeze. It was hunched over with its back to her, legs tucked up underneath it.

Bo's barking grew louder and more frantic.

It moved quickly, snapping around to face her. In the flashing blue of the lightning, she clearly saw a pasty-white chin, but the majority of the face was cloaked beneath a cowl. It cocked its head back and she saw lips stretched taut over yellowing teeth. Two white globes leered out at her from sockets that were framed by dried eyelids, which had been peeled back to either side. Both were slit down the center with ragged gashes like a cat's eyes, the resultant chasm filled with scabbed blood. Four long scars ran from the forehead through the brows, and then down the cheeks.

"Steve," she gasped.

She didn't even see him move.

There was only the coldness of the grave as those black tendrils wrapped around her and pulled her to him.

A flash of rusted metal and searing pain.

When the lightning faded, there was only a Labrador retriever barking at a patch of reeds.

And the echo of a scream dissipating over the marsh, before it was drowned out by a crash of thunder.

ABOUT THE AUTHOR

Michael McBride is the author of *Bloodletting*, *The Infected*, and the *God's End* trilogy. His short fiction has appeared in numerous anthologies and magazines, including *Dark Wisdom*, *Dark Discoveries*, and *Cemetery Dance*, which featured his story "It Rips," soon to be released as an independent film. He lives with his wife and four children in Westminster, Colorado, where he works as a radiologic technologist. To explore the author's other work or to contact him directly, please visit: www.michaelmcbride.net